SAMMY

AND THE

HEADLESS

HORSEMAN

SAMMY
AND THE
HEADLESS
HORSEMAN

RONA ARATO

Published in Canada by Fitzhenry & Whiteside, 195 Allstate Parkway, Markham, ON, L3R
4T8. Published in the U.S. in 2016 by Fitzhenry & Whiteside, 311 Washington Street, Brighton,
Massachusetts 02135.

www.fitzhenry.ca   godwit@fitzhenry.ca

10 9 8 7 6 5 4 3 2 1

We acknowledge with thanks the Canada Council for the Arts, and the Ontario Arts Council
for their support of our publishing program. We acknowledge the financial support of the
Government of Canada through the Canada Book Fund (CBF) for our publishing activities.

  ONTARIO ARTS COUNCIL
CONSEIL DES ARTS DE L'ONTARIO

Library and Archives Canada Cataloguing in Publication
Arato, Rona, author
       Sammy and the headless horseman / Rona Arato.
ISBN 978-1-55455-269-6 (paperback)
       I. Title.
PS8601.R35S24 2016   jC813'.6   C2015-907273-5

Publisher Cataloging-in-Publication Data (U.S.)
Arato, Rona.
Sammy and the Headless Horseman / Rona Arato.
Summary: "Eleven-year-old Sammy is stuck in the Catskill Mountains for the summer with
his awful cousin Joshua. Trouble seems to follow as Sammy becomes entangled in a series of
mysterious occurrences, including a terrifying headless horseman who seems to be haunting the
reclusive "Hermit" at the top of the neighboring hill. Set in the early 1920s, after WWI"
– Provided by publisher.
Identifiers: ISBN 978-1-55455-269-6 (hardcover)
Subjects: LCSH: Headless Horseman (Fictitious character) – Juvenile fiction. | Hotels -- Catskill
(N.Y.) – Juvenile fiction. | Detective and mystery stories.
Classification: LCC PZ7.A738Sa |DDC [FIC] – dc23

Cover and text design by Cheryl Chen
Cover art by Roshan Kurichiyanil
Printed in Canada

To my grandchildren

Cy, Samantha, Tali, and Simon:

this is your history too.

CHAPTER ONE

WELCOME TO THE CATSKILLS

"Beware the nights with a full moon. We have ghosts and dark spirits living in these Catskill Mountains." Adam Van Dorn grinned as he flicked the wagon horse's reins.

Sammy twisted on the hard wooden seat so he could look at Adam beside him. "Ghosts? You're joking, right? Are you trying to scare me?"

"Why? Do you get frightened easily?" The older boy smiled, but Sammy saw a hint of seriousness in his gray eyes. "The Catskills can be scary." Adam lowered his voice. "Some people even say the Pine Grove Hotel is haunted."

"Haunted?" Joshua leaned forward, his head jutting between Sammy and Adam. "By real ghosts?"

"Yeah, Joshua," Sammy replied. "You'd better watch out

or you might become one of them."

"You can't scare me, Sammy Levin! I'm way tougher than you."

Sammy's cousin, "the Awful Joshua," loved to make Sammy's life miserable, and this summer was no exception. Adam, on the other hand, seemed like he'd be fun to hang out with. At fourteen, Adam was two years older than Sammy. He had a shock of sandy hair beneath his cap and eyes that crinkled in the corners. Sammy admired the way he guided the horse with practiced ease.

"Joshua, sit back before you make yourself sick," barked Aunt Pearl.

Sammy sighed. His aunt was another burden he would have to bear. It had been a long trip and he was tired. First, there was the taxi ride from his home on Orchard Street to the ferry dock, then a ride across the Hudson River. Next was a two-hour train trip from New Jersey to the town of Liberty, New York. Aunt Pearl fussed the whole time about not being able to open the windows because the soot from the train would choke them. Adam had been waiting for them at the station. He'd introduced himself and had helped them into the wagon before setting off on the forty-five minute ride to the hotel.

"Here we are!" Adam dropped the reins and the horse whinnied. He helped Aunt Pearl climb down from the wagon, followed by Joshua and Leah, his six-year-old sister. "Welcome to the Pine Grove Hotel—the finest establishment in the Catskill Mountains."

Aunt Pearl peeled off her gloves, which were covered in coal dust from the train's smokestack. She was tall and stout. Her dark hair was streaked with gray, and when she was angry, she could freeze anyone with a glance of her ice-blue eyes. "Sammy, help Adam with the valises. Joshua, Leah, come with me." She turned towards the building.

Sammy looked at his cousin. "Hey, Joshua, why don't you carry some of this stuff too?"

"Because I don't have to." Joshua thumbed his nose.

Joshua was tall, like his mother, but skinny as a rail. His fair, straight hair and blue eyes were the opposite of Sammy's curly dark mop and brown eyes. Over the past year, Sammy had almost caught up to him in height but Joshua still topped him by an inch. *We don't even look like family*, Sammy thought and, not for the first time, almost wished they weren't.

"Sammy! Stop dreaming and let's go," Aunt Pearl ordered.

Boy oh boy, Sammy sighed as he picked up a valise. *This is going to be a long summer.*

They were met at the door by a girl about Adam's age with curly brown hair, a freckled face, and a wide, friendly smile. She held out a hand. "Here, let me help you."

"Who are you?" Joshua asked rudely.

The girl ignored him and turned to Aunt Pearl. "I'm Shayna Liebman. I'll be showing you to your room. Please follow me." She picked up a bag and turned towards the staircase.

Adam bounded up the stairs with Shayna and Sammy, a valise in each hand. "Shayna's parents own the Pine Grove. She works here in the summer like I do."

"Here we are, ma'am. This is your room," announced Shayna. She swung open the door to a large, airy room with one large bed and a sofa.

Sammy was confused. "Where do I sleep?"

"You're bunking with me," Adam said. "After we finish this, Shayna and I will show you the rest of the hotel."

That sounded like a lot more fun than hanging out with his aunt and cousin. This summer might turn out better than he'd thought.

While Aunt Pearl, Joshua, and Leah started settling in, Shayna, Adam, and Sammy took a walk. Shayna became the tour guide. They walked to a small bungalow across the lawn from the main building. It was one room, furnished with two beds, a small table, and two chairs. Sammy put down his suitcase and looked around.

"This is your bed." Adam pointed to the cot near the window. He pointed to a chest of drawers in the corner. "The bottom two drawers are yours and the bathroom is outside."

"Like in Poland," Sammy laughed.

Adam moved to the door. "Let's get on with the tour. You can unpack later."

The Pine Grove Hotel consisted of three buildings—a two-storey white frame house with a wide porch that stretched the length of its front and emerald green shutters and railings, a smaller house in the same style, and a one-storey white frame building with a porch.

"How long have your parents had the hotel?" Sammy asked Shayna as they stopped in front of the last building.

"It was my grandparents' farm. They bought it when they came to America from Hungary in 1880." Shayna sat on the steps leading to the porch. She motioned for the others to join her. "After my grandfather died, my grandmother started taking in boarders in the summer to help pay the bills. When she died, my uncle inherited the farm across the road and my mother the farmhouse, which is now the hotel."

"What is this building?" Sammy asked pointing behind them.

"It's the casino. My parents built it three years ago and it's where the nightly entertainment takes place."

Adam hooked his thumbs under the straps of his bright red suspenders. "During the week there are card games and discussions but on special nights, the casino comes alive. I'm in charge of the entertainment."

"With Moishe's help," Shayna added playfully.

"Who is Moishe?"

"Moishe is a *tummler*. An entertainer," Adam explained.

"What kind of entertainment do you have?"

"Singing. Jokes. Sometimes, we get stars from the Yiddish theatre in New York. Well, maybe not *stars*," Shayna added as Adam gave her a bemused look. "But good performers."

"Wow." Sammy was impressed. The Yiddish theatre

was the cultural centre of the Lower East Side. Earlier this year, for his birthday, his Aunt Tsippi had taken him to see the great Yiddish actor, Boris Thomashefsky, acting as Hamlet. He didn't like the play—too many people died—but he had been captivated by Mr. Thomashefsky's acting. Suddenly Sammy had another thought. "Is there a piano?"

"Yes."

"Who plays it?"

"I do," Shayna said proudly. "I know all the popular songs."

"Do people sing?"

Adam gave Sammy a startled look. "Why? Do you want to put on a show? How old are you?"

"I'm eleven and no." Sammy's cheeks got hot. "I just…I like singing."

They walked back to the main building and went inside. Shayna showed Sammy the parlor, dining room, and kitchen. "There are six bedrooms, two downstairs and four upstairs."

"There you are." Aunt Pearl was standing in the lobby with Joshua on one side of her and Leah on the other. She was tapping her foot—a sure sign that she was annoyed. She explained that Sammy was sleeping in a bungalow because he was hired help.

"Hired help?" Sammy looked at her in surprise. "You mean I'm working here?"

"Just a few hours a day," said Aunt Pearl. "To pay your expenses."

"Does Papa know you brought me up here to work?"

"Sammy, darling." Aunt Pearl looked down her rather prominent nose. "I am not sending you to dig coal in a mine. Just a little help in the kitchen here and there. Besides," she said, pointing to Adam and Shayna, "I'm sure you'll be much happier with young people like yourself than with us upstairs.

To that, Sammy had no argument. Even the coal mine sounded better than staying with Aunt Pearl and the Awful Joshua.

"Adam," Aunt Pearl turned to him. "Will you show Sammy where he will sleep?"

"I've already done that." Adam turned to Sammy. "You're going to like life in the bungalow."

"Where do you stay?" Sammy asked Shayna.

"I live with my parents in the house near the swimming pool. I have to go now, but I'll see you later."

"Joshua, Leah! Time to wash up. We will see you for

dinner, Sammy. Do *not* be late." Aunt Pearl swiftly turned on her heel and started towards the stairs.

"Bye, Thammy." Leah waved as Sammy and Adam walked to the door.

"Bye, Leah." Sammy blew her a kiss. He liked Leah. Too bad she was stuck with Joshua for a brother.

"Bye, Sammy." Joshua pinched his nose. "*I* think *you* stink. Go jump in the *lake* for our noses' *sake*."

"Is that your cousin?" Adam asked as he and Sammy crossed the grass between the main building and a cluster of one-storey white bungalows.

"Yeah." Sammy kicked at a clump of dirt. "That's the Awful Joshua."

"Bad luck." Adam laughed. "How did you end up coming here?"

"My Aunt Pearl thought it'd be good for me. I have a gang in New York and she thinks I'd just get into trouble over the summer."

"Would you?"

"Well, not on purpose. In order to join the gang, I had to steal something from Kaufman's Five Cent Store. I got caught and was almost arrested, but the store manager offered me a job instead. I was able to trick the rest of the gang into working there too."

"Wow, that's pretty amazing." Adam laughed. "Do your parents approve of your gang?"

"My dad likes them enough."

"And your mom?"

Sammy paused. "She died. My dad just got married again. I don't know anything about my stepmom, but that's another reason Aunt Pearl dragged me out here. She said they should 'be alone to get to know each other.'" He mimicked his aunt's high-pitched voice.

"Try to ignore your aunt and you'll like it here."

"Do you live here?"

"My family lives in Monticello, about ten miles from Loch Sheldrake. For the past two years, I've worked here in the summer."

"So what's your job?" Sammy asked Adam.

"I do just about everything. I drive the wagon, work in the kitchen, I'm the lifeguard at the pool and,"—he puffed out his chest—"like I told you, I'm the social director. I organize the games and the entertainment. Especially on important days, like the Fourth of July. And," he gave Sammy a wicked grin, "I do a bit of hunting."

Hunting? "What kind of hunting?"

"The best kind." Adam arched his eyebrows. "Ghost-hunting."

Now he was talking. Before Sammy could ask for more details, an angry scream came from the main house.

CHAPTER TWO

A NEW JOB

The boys ran into the front room to find a woman wringing her hands and staring at a picture on the wall. She was stout with red cheeks, crinkly blue eyes, and gray hair pulled into a tight knot at the back of her head.

"Mrs. Liebman, are you okay? What happened?" Adam asked as he and Sammy rushed over to her.

"She cut me out. See?" She pointed. "It's our wedding picture but she cut me out of it."

Sammy looked at the photograph. Sure enough, there was a slash through the image of the bride.

"It's her—I know it! She's doing this to scare me. Well, I will not have it!" she said. "She can ruin all the pictures she wants."

"Who?" asked Sammy.

"Mrs. Liebman, this is Sammy. He's here for the summer."

"Oh, it's nice to meet you, Sammy." She wiped her eyes with the corner of her white apron. "Oy, so much commotion! Adam, lay out the tablecloths while I finish cooking, please."

"Of course." Adam grabbed the tablecloths from a nearby cupboard as Mrs. Liebman headed back into the kitchen.

"Who was she talking about, Adam?" Sammy asked as they walked into the dining room.

"Her grandmother."

"Oh, where is she?"

"She died twenty years ago."

"What? Then how can she ruin a photograph?"

"Mrs. Liebman thinks she haunts the hotel."

"That doesn't make sense."

"I told you we had ghosts," Adam said, straightening the last tablecloth. "I'm going to help out in the kitchen. You're eating in the dining room tonight. I'll see you later."

The hotel dining room was a cheerful space with windows overlooking the porch on one side and a wall covered with framed photographs on the other. The twelve guests sat around a long table in the middle of the room. Three other tables stood against the wall. Mrs. Liebman explained that they were for the guests who would arrive later and stay for the July Fourth week. Sammy took a seat next to Joshua. Aunt Pearl informed him that he could eat with them tonight because he didn't officially start work until the morning. Sammy could hear his father's voice: *She's no better than us, Sammy. Ignore her.* Of course *he* didn't have to spend the summer with her!

Sammy looked around the table at the other guests. The man across from him introduced himself as Mr. Katzenblum, a thin fidgety man in a white summer suit, white shirt, and red bow tie. He wore a single eyeglass on his left eye, which he called a monocle, that was attached to a chain that hooked onto his belt. A wooden cane with a silver handle and a tip in the shape of a claw was propped by his chair.

Next to Mr. Katzenblum was a plump woman. She introduced herself as Mrs. Weiss. Her five-year-old daughter Esther, and her baby son David sat beside her. Mrs. Weiss and Esther both had red hair. Mrs. Weiss' hair was folded into a hairnet at the nape of her neck, while Esther's fell in an unruly tumble of curls to her shoulders. Mrs. Weiss' thirteen-year-old niece Naomi was trying to feed David who was bouncing up and down in his wooden high chair.

"Naomi, don't let him play with his food," Mrs. Weiss scolded. "Food is for eating. We should only have had such food in Poland."

Naomi pushed a lock of black hair off her forehead. "He's not hungry, Aunt Sarah."

"Then take the food away."

Naomi lifted David's hand from the dish of mashed carrots and set the dish on the table. She wet her napkin with water from her glass and washed the baby's hands and face.

Sammy leaned over and whispered to Naomi, "What crime did you commit to come here?"

"Poor relative."

"Me too." He held out his hand as if begging. They both laughed.

On Sammy's other side was a woman from New York who informed him that he could call her Molly. Molly had silver hair in two braids piled on the top of her head. She ate with a sharp mincing motion, chewing each mouthful thoroughly, then daintily dabbing her lips with a white linen napkin.

"So, young man, where you are from?" she asked after everyone had eaten the first course—a thick cabbage soup.

"New York," Sammy answered.

"*Everyone* is from New York. *Before* New York, I mean." She paused for breath as Shayna placed plates of roast beef brisket, boiled potatoes, and tiny green peas in front of them.

The aroma made Sammy's mouth water. He dug into the beef. The papery thin slices oozed gravy and melted on his tongue. He reached for a hunk of fresh baked bread to soak up the gravy.

"So, young man? Speak up. I can't hear you." Molly leaned towards Sammy and placed a small silver horn to her ear.

"Poland," he shouted into the horn.

"Don't shout! I'm not deaf," she shouted. "I am from Hungary, Budapest," she said in a voice filled with pride. "A very cultured city. Not like New York."

"If it's so cultured, why did you leave?"

"Why does anyone leave?" She sighed, placed the horn in her lap, and turned to Mr. Katzenblum. "Is your room nice?" Molly asked.

Mr. Katzenblum dabbed at his lips with a white linen napkin. "Reasonably. Although, one window is blocked by a tree and the only thing I can see out of the other is a rundown cabin up on the hill."

Molly turned to Leah. "And do you like your room, my dear?"

Leah smiled. "Yeth," she lisped through the gap in her teeth. "Mama and I have a big bed and Joshua thleeps on the thofa."

I hope it has springs that poke his back, Sammy thought as Shayna served slabs of sponge cake soaked with honey and covered with fresh strawberries.

"Wow." Sammy rubbed his stomach as they got up from the table. "That was delicious."

"The way you ate, it's a good thing they're not charging us by the pound," Aunt Pearl grumbled.

"Such a healthy appetite is good to see." Mrs. Liebman walked up to them. "Not like this one, picking at his food." Mrs. Liebman turned to Joshua. "You maybe do not like my cooking?"

"Joshua always pickths at his food," said Leah. "That's why he's tho thin."

Joshua's cheeks flamed. "Everything is delicious, Mrs. Liebman. I just can't eat like a pig like some people…"

"Please, this is a kosher hotel. Pigs, we do not allow."

Mrs. Liebman laughed. "So, you will be helping me in the kitchen tomorrow." Mrs. Liebman looked Sammy up and down. Suddenly, a tall, stocky man barged into the room.

"I warned you to keep your guests on your side of the road!" he shouted.

"What's this about, Nathan?"

He pointed to Naomi. "You want flowers? Pick them in the woods, not on my farm. Next time…" he waved his fist in the air.

"I'm sorry, Mr. Rothstein…I didn't…I wasn't…" Naomi stammered.

Mrs. Liebman put a hand on Naomi's shoulder. "Don't worry, child. You are not in trouble." She turned to her brother. "So, again with the threats?"

Mr. Rothstein pulled his bushy brows together and glared at her. "We made a deal, Rose. Keep your…" he spat out the word, "*customers* on your side of the property. And off of mine!" He turned on his heel and stormed out the door.

Mrs. Liebman sighed. She turned to Naomi who looked like she was about to cry. "You didn't do anything wrong. But stay away from his farm—for your sake, not his. Now," she turned back to Sammy. "Adam has showed you where you will sleep?"

"Yes." Sammy nodded. Suddenly he was glad that he would work with this good-natured woman who made such delicious food, even if she did believe in ghosts and have an angry brother.

"Good." Mrs. Liebman patted his shoulder. "Tomorrow morning I will show you what to do."

"Okay. I'll be ready."

"That's settled. Now go outside and enjoy."

Sammy found Adam waiting on the porch. "Come," he motioned. "I want to show you something."

Sammy followed his new friend across the grass to a clump of trees. Although it was almost eight o'clock, the sky was still blue with wispy clouds streaked pink. Adam pushed through the underbrush. Occasionally they stopped to eat raspberries that grew on bushes along the path.

"Tomorrow we can come and fill buckets with them," said Adam as they wiped red juice from their chins. "There are blueberries too. Mrs. Liebman will put them into pies. Come on."

Sammy followed and soon they were standing before a lake.

"This is our private swimming hole." Adam spread his

arms wide. "The hotel guests swim in the pool behind the main building."

Sammy dipped his hand into the water. It was cool and felt like silk against his skin. "Adam, look." A mother duck was shepherding her brood of four fuzzy ducklings into the water.

"They hatched last week." Adam grinned. "You know what that means?"

"What?"

"Duck soup." Adam rubbed his hands together.

"No!"

"I'm only joking."

"What's that noise?" Sammy cocked his head.

"That croaking? Frogs. They live in the lake too. See, there's one." Adam pointed to a clump of reeds at the water's edge. "Its colour camouflages it so it blends in with the reeds."

Sammy squinted. "Yeah, I see it."

"And this is the hotel's newest addition." Adam walked over to a wooden dock. "The Liebmans built this last summer to reach the deep part of the lake where there are fish." He pointed to a rowboat tied to one of the dock's pilings. "I like to row out to the middle of the lake but sometimes I fish off the end of the dock. And it makes a great diving board when we swim here. We can try it out tomorrow."

Sammy lowered his head. "I can't, I mean, I don't want to…" Sammy thought of himself thrashing around in the water when he had fallen into the ocean at Ellis Island, while waiting to get into New York after the journey from Poland. He'd thought he would drown until his sister Malka pulled him out. Since then Sammy had been terrified of trying to swim.

"You don't swim?" Adam looked at him in surprise. Then his expression brightened. "That's all right. I can teach you. But the lake isn't the real attraction. That is." He turned and pointed to a cabin on top of the hill behind the main building. "That's where the Hermit lives."

"Hermit? What is that?"

"You mean *who*. The Hermit is a cranky old man who lives all alone. Rumour has it that he's being terrorized by a nasty ghost. You and me," Adam said, turning to Sammy, "we're going to catch it."

"What? How?"

"I'm counting on you to help me figure that out."

"Why don't we catch the hotel ghost instead? Or is it

the same ghost?"

"I think Mrs. Liebman's just imagining things. But the Hermit's ghost is real." Adam looked up at the sky. "We'd better get back. It will be dark soon and the mosquitoes will eat us alive. We've got an early start tomorrow."

Later, in bed, the whole incredible day spun around in Sammy's head like the spots in a kaleidoscope. Here he was, lying on a cot in a strange bungalow in the Catskill Mountains, his stomach full of fresh berries, and his brain filled with questions. Was there really a ghost haunting the hotel? Who was the Hermit? Why was Mr. Rothstein so mad at his sister? What was the gang back home doing? A cool breeze blew through the bungalow's window and Sammy thought of Papa and Malka in the sweltering heat of New York City. Malka was expecting a baby in August. *I hope she's not too uncomfortable. Maybe she and her husband can come up for a visit. Papa too. I will write to them tomorrow.*

CHAPTER THREE

SPILLED EGGS

"Wake up, sleepy head."

Sammy opened his eyes. For a moment he didn't remember where he was and then Adam shook his shoulder.

"The rooster crowed and Mrs. Liebman's waiting for us in the kitchen."

"What time is it?" Sammy yawned.

"Five thirty."

"Five thirty! That's the middle of the night." He closed his eyes.

"Not here it isn't. We have to set up for breakfast. C'mon." Adam pulled Sammy's blanket off, tossed him a towel, and led him outside to the water pump. As Sammy splashed cold water on his face, he thought of the day ahead and became excited.

As they entered the kitchen, Mrs. Liebman was pulling loaves of fragrant bread from the oven of the coal-burning stove. Her cheeks were flushed from the heat and beads of sweat dotted her forehead.

"Good morning, you two. *Oy.*" She put her hand at the small of her back and stretched. "My back aches. Mixing dough, kneading dough, and pulling pots and pans in and out of the oven—even my bones hurt."

"We could come earlier and help you," Sammy suggested.

"Don't even think of it." Adam poked him in the side.

"Ouch. Why not?"

"She might take you up on it. Besides," he whispered, "these are her two favourite things: baking and complaining."

"So?" Mrs. Liebman stepped in front of them, hands on her hips. "You are going to maybe talk all day while the breakfast table stays empty?"

Adam snapped to attention. "No, ma'am. We're ready to work."

"Okay. But first you eat." She looked Sammy up and down. "Such a nice looking boy. *Pooh, pooh, pooh.* But too thin." She handed each of the boys a plate with a warm bun cut in half and spread thick with butter. "Sit." She pointed to the round table, which was covered with a red-and-white checkered oilcloth. Sammy gobbled up the bun, then had another, and washed them down with a glass of creamy milk still warm from the cow.

"Milked her myself." Adam pantomimed milking a cow.

"We had a cow in Poland. Her name was *Nudnik*. That means 'pest'."

"I know what it means. That's what Mrs. Liebman calls me when I ask too many questions." He gave Sammy a puzzled look. "Mrs. Liebman gave you a compliment and then said '*pooh, pooh, pooh*'. She does that a lot. What does it mean?"

Sammy laughed. "It's a Jewish thing. To ward off," he lowered his voice, "the evil eye. My grandmother did it too. She would spit on the floor three times. My mother said that was disgusting so she would just say '*pooh, pooh, pooh*' to pretend she was spitting."

"Thanks for explaining it. Come on." He took their empty plates and glasses to the sink. "We have to set the table for breakfast." Adam walked over to a row of cupboards on the wall opposite the sink. "These are the dairy dishes." He opened the door and pointed to stacks of white plates, bowls, and cups in the first cupboard. "The meat dishes are in here." He moved to the next cupboard. "They have red flowers on them so you can tell them apart."

"We keep kosher at home," Sammy said. "I know that meat and dairy dishes and pots are kept separate, and you don't serve milk with meat."

"You have to be really careful not to mix them up." Adam closed the door to the meat cupboard. "Mrs. Liebman is really strict about that."

"So is my father," Sammy reassured him. "I'll be fine. Where's your family from?" he asked as they put on their aprons.

"My family's Dutch. They came here from the Netherlands almost a hundred years ago," Adam said proudly. "Many Dutch people settled in the Catskills. My father's a doctor in Monticello."

"What does 'Catskills' mean?" The name had been puzzling Sammy ever since he'd first heard it.

"My father says that *kill* is Dutch for 'creek'. He thinks the explorer Henry Hudson named it *Cats kill* for the bobcats that lived nearby. But no one really knows."

"Why do you work here?"

"I earn extra money. I like the Liebmans. The guests are nice. And it's fun." He paused. "Do you believe in that evil eye stuff?"

"Not really."

"Mrs. Liebman thinks her dead grandmother is angry because she's using her recipes."

Sammy stared at him. "That is ridiculous."

"Is it?" Adam raised an eyebrow. "Weirder things have happened in these mountains."

When Sammy asked him what he meant, he waved the question away. "Time to get to work."

Sammy followed Adam into the dining room. They set out a white china plate, a cup and saucer, and a fork, knife, and spoon at each place. Shayna came in with pitchers of sour cream, which she placed at opposite ends of the table. By the time they finished, the guests were coming down for breakfast.

"You mean I have to serve Joshua?" Sammy wailed to Adam.

"Good morning, Sammy." Aunt Pearl marched into the dining room, her white dress billowing behind her like a ship's sails. Leah skipped beside her. She wore a white pinafore with yellow polka dots, white shoes, yellow socks, and yellow-and-white striped ribbons on her honey-coloured pigtails. Joshua was right behind her, wearing short blue pants held up by red-and-white suspenders, and a short-sleeved white shirt. "And how did you sleep last night?" Aunt Pearl asked as Sammy pulled out her chair.

"Fine, thank you, Aunt Pearl."

"Hi, Thammy." Leah tugged at Sammy's apron.

"Hi, Toothless." He yanked one of her braids.

"I'm not all toothleth," she giggled.

"Leah, sit down," Aunt Pearl ordered. "You too, Joshua."

"I want to go swimming after breakfast," Joshua said.

"We shall see." Aunt Pearl shook out the white linen napkin and placed it across her broad lap. "Oh dear. I forgot my shawl. Sammy, darling, be a good boy and get Joshua and Leah orange juice and bring me a cup of tea while I go back to my room."

Sammy looked at Adam and rolled his eyes.

"Good morning, Sammy." Molly slid into the chair next to where Sammy had sat as a guest the night before. "So, today you are my waiter?"

"Yes, Mrs., err…Molly. Would you like orange juice?"

"Adam, I can't do this," Sammy said when they were in the kitchen loading round metal trays with plates of herring and boiled eggs.

"Remember the ghost-hunting," Adam said. Lifting the tray high with his right hand, he walked to the swinging doors that separated the kitchen from the dining room. Pushing the doors open with his hip, he sauntered through, balancing the tray on the palm of his hand.

Sammy picked up a tray and held it with his right hand while he placed his left palm underneath. Raising it above his head, he imitated Adam and swung through the kitchen doors. As he did so, he lost his balance and the tray slipped forward, sending dishes clattering over the edge and onto the floor. Cracked eggs rolled across the room, oozing streams of yellow yolk. Chunks of herring, swimming in sour cream, carpeted the floor while the egg cups rolled back and forth like a crazy game of marbles.

"Aaagh!" Sammy looked up and saw Aunt Pearl, who had just come in from the front room, slip in the goo and slide across the floor. Her feet flew up from under her and she landed *splat* in a puddle of egg yolk.

Sammy leaned against the wall, horrified at the mess. Aunt Pearl was screaming. Shayna and Adam rushed over, grabbed her arms and pulled her, painfully, to her feet. Leah patted the yellow spots on her mother's arm with a napkin.

Joshua laughed. "Mom. Now your dress matches Leah's polka dots."

At that moment, Mrs. Liebman walked into the room. Surveying the mess, she turned to Sammy and sighed. "*Boychik,* please, for lunch, do me a favor and hold the tray with *two* hands."

"Did you see my aunt sitting in the egg yolks?" Sammy grinned as he and Adam walked to the lake. "I wish I had a picture."

"Your aunt didn't think it was funny." Adam shook his head and then laughed. "But I sure did. I'll show you how to hold the tray on the palm of your hand, but you have to promise to carry it with two hands until you learn."

"I promise," Sammy said. "So, tell me more about the Hermit."

They stopped by a tree and Adam motioned for them to sit down. "Do you know the story of "Rip Van Winkle?""

"No. Who was he?"

Adam crossed his legs so they were tucked tailor style under him. He leaned forward, balancing his chin on his fisted hands. "The story goes that Rip Van Winkle had this mean old wife who always nagged him. So one night he went up in the hills and disappeared."

"Disappeared?"

"Uh huh. Everyone in his village thought he was dead. His wife had to work and his children grew up. People forgot about him. Then one day, he came back with a long white beard down to here." Adam pointed to his waist. He leaned forward, widened his eyes, and stared at Sammy. "He had been asleep for twenty years!"

"Twenty years!" Sammy gasped. "That's impossible."

"That is what all the villagers thought. But it was true."

"When did this happen?"

"Almost 150 years ago."

"What does that have to do with the Hermit?"

"Nothing. But it's a good story. Washington Irving wrote it. He was an author who loved the Catskills and wrote about them."

"Adam! What about the Hermit?"

Adam laughed. "Well, sometimes I see him when he goes into town for food or to pick up his mail. And he takes care of the Pine Grove in the winter, when the Liebmans are in the city."

"Why do they call him a hermit, then?"

"He doesn't come down in the summer, when there are lots of people around. In the winter, he's here by himself." He paused. "Well, except for Mr. Rothstein, Mrs. Liebman's brother. He owns the farm across the road. But Mr. Rothstein and Mrs. Liebman don't talk to each other."

"He was yelling at her last night. Why is he so angry?"

"It has something to do with who owns the farm and who owns the hotel. The hotel belonged to their mother. She was a widow and ran it with the help of her son and daughter. But it was the daughter—Mrs. Liebman—who really helped her. When their mother died, she left the hotel to Mrs. Liebman and Mr. Rothstein hasn't spoken to her since. My father says it's a shame when family members can't get along. Like you and your cousin."

"Yeah, well, Joshua doesn't make it easy."

"Forget about being stuck with him. We're going to have some fun this summer." Adam's eyes gleamed with excitement as he stared up at the cabin. "The ghost that's haunting the Hermit is a mystery, Sammy—a great unsolved mystery, which you and I are going to figure out. But first," he sighed, as he got to his feet, "we have to set the table for lunch."

CHAPTER FOUR

A TRIP TO TOWN

"Come on, Sammy. We have to go into town to get Mrs. Liebman's groceries. You might even see the Hermit," said Adam as he led Sammy to the stable.

"Who's the Hermit?"

Sammy spun around. "Joshua, don't sneak up on us like that."

"I didn't sneak up. I walked by. So, when are we leaving?"

"Not *we*." Adam crooked a finger in Sammy's direction. "*Us*. Sammy and me."

Joshua turned to the door. "I'm going to tell my mother you're being mean to me."

"Wait." Sammy grabbed his arm and sighed. "Adam, how are we getting into town?"

"In the wagon. I bring back the supplies. Flour." He

pantomimed lifting a heavy bag. "Great big sacks of flour."

"Can you carry a heavy sack, Joshua?"

"You bet I can." Joshua flexed his muscles. "I'm strong."

"I'll bet you are," Adam muttered under his breath. "Okay, you can come. But only on one condition."

"What's that?"

Adam bent down so his face was level with Joshua's. "I'm the boss. You listen to me and do what I say. Deal?"

"Deal." Joshua grasped Adam's hand and pumped it up and down. "This is going to be fun," he gloated.

Sammy very much doubted that.

Adam leaned down from the wagon seat. "All right you two. We have to get going so we'll be back in time to set the tables for dinner."

"I don't have to set the table. *I'm* a guest," said Joshua.

"Like mother, like son." Adam shook his head.

The ride to town was shorter than when Adam had picked Sammy and his family up at the train station in the town of Liberty. Loch Sheldrake was a village about two miles from the Pine Grove. It had a main street with a general store, a café, a dry goods store, and a barbershop. Adam stopped the wagon in front of Klein's General Store and Post Office. He climbed down and tied the horse's reins to the post in front of the store. He pulled a sugar cube from his pocket. The horse nuzzled his hand then whinnied. "Good boy, Simon."

Joshua made a face. "Your horse is named Simon?"

"The man we bought him from named him after his uncle."

"If you get a horse, Sammy, you can name him Milton." Joshua hooted.

"I'd rather name it after you."

"Hey!" Joshua followed Sammy and Adam up the steps and into the store.

As the wooden door slammed behind them, Sammy felt a whoosh of dusty air hit his face. The inside was crowded with boxes of canned foods, sacks of flour, and barrels of sour pickles. A wooden counter ran from the front window to the back wall. Behind it were shelves filled with jars of coffee, tea, and spices. A woman in a flowered cotton dress was watching a man weigh sugar. He poured a scoop into one of the scales and placed a round piece of metal on the other. When he was done, he poured the sugar into a brown paper sack, twisted the top shut, and handed it to a woman. "That'll be five cents, Mrs. Shapiro.

Will there be anything else?"

"No thank you, Mr. Klein." The woman opened her handbag, took out a nickel and handed it to him. She accepted the sugar and with a nod at the boys, left the store.

"That lady comes in every day. One time it's five cents worth of sugar, another it's a quarter-pound of butter. Never buys more than one thing at a time." Mr. Klein shook his head.

"Maybe she doesn't like to carry a lot of groceries," said Adam. "Maybe she could use a delivery boy." He poked his thumb at his chest.

"No. I think she's lonely and just looking for an excuse for company." Mr. Klein leaned over the counter. "Now what can I do for you today? And who are your friends?"

"This is Sammy. He's up for the summer. And that," Adam pointed, "is his cousin Joshua."

"Pleased to meet you." Sammy held out his hand.

"Pleased to meet you too, Sammy." Mr. Klein smiled and shook his hand. He was a big man with a shiny bald head, glasses, a round face, and an even rounder belly. When he smiled a gold tooth winked in the corner of his mouth. "So, boys, you've come up to the mountains to work?" He rubbed his fingers together. "Earn a little *gelt*?" he said, using the Yiddish word for money.

"Sammy's working. *I'm* a guest." Joshua folded his arms across his chest.

"I see." Mr. Klein looked at Sammy. "Welcome to the Catskills."

"Mrs. Liebman has a long list for you today." Adam pulled a crumpled piece of paper from his pants pocket, smoothed it on the counter, and handed it to Mr. Klein.

"Hmm, expecting a crowd, is she?"

"Next week is the Fourth of July."

"So it is." Mr. Klein drummed his fingers on the countertop. "Okay, boys. Stay put while I fill the order." He turned and then hoisted a sack of flour onto the counter. At that moment, the door swung open and a tall man with coffee-coloured skin, shaggy gray hair, and a scar on his left cheek entered. He was wearing denim overalls, a red-and-black checked shirt, and mud-caked leather boots.

Adam poked Sammy. "That's the Hermit," he whispered.

Joshua's eyes bulged.

"Don't stare," Adam hissed.

"But he's a N-negro."

Adam slapped a hand over Joshua's mouth.

"Mornin', Mr. Klein." The man lumbered up to the counter. "Got any mail for me today?"

"'Fraid not, Zeke."

The man frowned. "You sure? You go back and check that sack of mail again."

"I've emptied it and I can assure you, there's nothin' in there for you. Unless you'd like to take Mrs. Rosen her Sears and Roebuck catalogue."

The Hermit smiled a big toothy smile. "In that case, I'll just take four eggs."

"Eggs? What's wrong with your chickens? You scared them out of layin'?"

The Hermit's expression turned grim. "Someone or something got to my chickens. Same's they trampled my vegetable patch the week before." He leaned over the counter and lowered his voice. "Some fool hidin' his head in a black cape and ridin' a horse."

"Maybe it's *the* Headless Horseman that's haunting you," joked Mr. Klein. "You know, the one from the story."

"Ain't no such things as ghosts. But these attacks are happening more often."

"Have you told Sheriff Miller?"

"What am I gonna tell him? 'You see, Sheriff, there's

this guy without a head ridin' around scarin' my chickens.' He'll think I'm plumb crazy."

The sound of a stifled giggle made the Hermit turn around and glare at Joshua. "What you laughin' at, boy? You think a man bein' terrorized is funny?"

"No. No, sir." Joshua clapped a hand over his mouth. "I mean…"

The Hermit turned back to Mr. Klein. "I'll come back another time, when there ain't no laughin' fools to put up with." He stomped out of the store and slammed the door behind him.

Mr. Klein frowned at Joshua. Before he could say anything, the door banged open and a man barged in. Sammy had never seen anyone like him. He had leathery skin, squinty eyes, and a crooked nose that looked like it had been broken. His mouth was a slit in his shaggy beard. "I seen that darkie outside," he growled. "Pity when decent folks have to put up with his kind."

Mr. Klein came around the counter. "I thought I told you to stay out of my store, Amos. It's *your* kind, with your hateful talk, that I don't want here."

"I got as much right as him to be here." He spat on the floor.

"I'll have none of that," said Mr. Klein. "Read that." He pointed to a sign above the counter. "What does it say?"

Amos looked at it and squinted. "It says, uh, it says... Who cares what it says!"

"It says 'no spitting.' You can't read it, can you? Now get out of my store."

Amos sneered. "Make me."

"All right, Amos. That's enough!"

Everyone turned as a man in a uniform with a star on his chest came into the store. "Get out and stay out before I lock you up." He grabbed Amos's arm and guided him towards the door.

"You can't lock me up. I ain't done nothin' wrong. You ain't heard the last of me!" Amos shouted as he slammed the door behind him.

"Good riddance." Mr. Klein brushed his hands together. "You came here just in time. Boys, this is Sheriff Miller. Sheriff, these boys work for the Liebmans."

"I don't work. I'm a guest," Joshua corrected.

"Nice to meet you, boys." The sheriff turned to Mr. Klein. "You okay?"

"Yeah, I'm all right. It's Zeke I worry about. That man has put up with more than you'll ever imagine. It's those mountain men."

"What are mountain men?" Sammy gave him a quizzical look.

Mr. Klein pushed his glasses up on his forehead. "They are two brothers who live in a shack on top of the mountain. No one knows much about them, except that they live off the land. They keep to themselves. Stay away from them, boys. They're bad news."

Adam snapped his fingers. "Speaking of news, I almost forgot. Is there a letter for Mrs. Weiss or Mr. Katzenblum?"

Mr. Klein shook his head. "Not today. Don't know why everyone is so anxious to get letters. You'd think they were getting money."

"Maybe they are," Adam laughed. "Thanks, Mr. Klein."

"Joshua, what *were* you laughing about? "Adam demanded as he loaded the groceries into the wagon.

"The Headless Horseman stealing the Hermit's chickens."

"He was scaring them, not stealing them, but what's funny about that?" Sammy shot his cousin an evil look.

"If he hasn't got a head, how's he gonna eat them?"

Sammy slapped his forehead. "You are an idiot, Joshua."

"No, I'm not. If you don't have a head, you don't have a mouth, and if you don't have a mouth, how…?"

"We get it, Joshua," said Adam. "Now get this stuff in the wagon. If I don't get back soon, Mrs. Liebman'll have *my* head."

CHAPTER FIVE

THE HERMIT

"So, what do you think of the Hermit?" Adam asked. He and Sammy were setting the table for dinner as Joshua sat and watched.

"I think he's kind of cranky. And a little scary." Sammy set water glasses at each place.

"Mrs. Liebman says he used to be a slave."

"A slave?" Sammy took a stack of dinner plates from the sideboard and set them out.

"Yeah. Someone owned him." Adam flicked the cloth he was using to wipe the soup spoons. "Like the Liebmans own Simon the horse."

"The Hermit isn't a horse. He's a person. How do you *own* another person?"

Adam shrugged. "Mrs. Liebman says his owner beat

him. That's how he got the scar on his cheek. He ran away."

"Is that why he's being terrorized?" Joshua asked. "Maybe his owner wants him back?"

Adam looked at him in disgust. "He can't get him back, Joshua. There's no more slavery. Whatever the reason, someone or something is trying to scare the Hermit away."

"That's not right." Sammy remembered the soldiers riding through his village in Poland, their horses trampling the ground. People ran from the sound of their hooves and the soldiers' guns. "We came to America to get away from being scared all the time. We need to help him."

"I don't think he'd be too keen on a visit from us. Or people in general. He's a hermit, remember?" said Adam.

"We'll do it without him knowing. Like guardian angels," replied Sammy.

"Joshua! Where are you? If you want to swim, you need to do so before dinner." called Aunt Pearl from the front room.

"Coming!" Joshua shouted back, getting up from his chair. "Whew! Being a guest is hard work." He threw them a smug smile and skipped out of the room.

Adam rolled his eyes. "You sure you're related?"

Sammy sighed. "Any chance the Liebmans would adopt me?"

CHAPTER SIX

A SWIMMING LESSON

"Adam, you said the Hermit is being haunted, but he said he doesn't believe in ghosts."

"Someone is terrorizing him. Whether it's a ghost or not…" Adam shrugged. "Either way, I think we should help him."

"Me too." Sammy paused. "But what if he doesn't want our help?" Sammy ran a hand through his mop of dark hair. "We'd just be meddling."

Adam looked Sammy up and down. "From what you've told me about your gang, you don't mind meddling."

Sammy laughed. "I guess you're right."

"We need to go up to his cabin and investigate," said Adam.

Before he could think any more about the Hermit,

however, Sammy had much to learn about his work around the hotel. He and Adam got up early, gathered eggs from the henhouse, and then went into the kitchen to serve breakfast. After many tries, Sammy learned how to carry a tray through the kitchen's swinging doors, avoiding any more dining room disasters.

Between meals, he helped Adam with his tasks, learned his way around the hotel, and got to know the Liebmans. Shayna's parents worked in their bakery on Clinton Street from September to May. Mrs. Liebman baked bread, bagels, and pastries while her husband ran the bakery. Then, during the first week of June, the family moved to the hotel for the summer.

"What about the bakery?" Sammy asked Adam as they set the table for dinner. "Do they just close it?"

"They have people who run it for them. Mr. Liebman comes up in the middle of June to remove fallen tree branches, rake up dead leaves, and clean the swimming pool. I help him after school. Mrs. Liebman and Shayna scrub every inch of the hotel. Mrs. Liebman scours the pots and pans, and she and Shayna wash and iron all the curtains and linens. When everything is spotless, they open their door to welcome guests."

"Don't your parents mind you coming here?" Sammy asked as they walked to the swimming pool. He was wearing his blue short pants and a white shirt. Adam wore a black swimming costume. It was one piece with shoulder straps and pant legs halfway to his knees.

"They're happy to get rid of me for two months," Adam said. "They think that working here is good experience." He went on to explain that most of the guests were women and children who came to the hotel for the whole summer. Their husbands joined them on weekends, but during the week the women enjoyed gossiping and playing cards on the front porch while the children played on the tree-shaded lawn.

"It doesn't seem fair that the women are here, but the men have to work in the city," Sammy said to Adam.

"Mrs. Liebman says the men don't mind going back because it gives them a chance to be on their own for a few days." Adam winked. "Think of living with your Aunt Pearl all the time."

"Aagh!" Sammy wrapped his hand around his throat.

The swimming pool was behind the guest bungalows. It was rectangular with a cement bottom and sides and filled with cold, clear water that bubbled up from a natural underground spring. A rope strung through three large rubber balls bobbed across the middle, separating the shallow from the deep end.

Adam was the lifeguard and every afternoon at two, he conducted a swimming lesson in the shallow end. It was to this lesson that Sammy, with a white towel draped over his shoulder, was headed. He was hot and sweaty. The water in the pool looked cool and inviting after the heat of the kitchen. He leaned over and ran his fingers in the water. Then he took a deep breath, closed his eyes, and, clutching his knees to his chest, jumped into the water. Too late, he realized he was in the deep end of the pool. His shirt billowed out like a balloon. He'd forgotten to take off his shoes and they felt like lead weights pulling his feet down. Gathering all his strength, he kicked the cement bottom and used his arms to propel himself to the surface.

"He's going to drown!" Sammy heard Aunt Pearl scream as his head broke through the water. Gasping for breath, Sammy flailed his arms and kicked with his legs. He sank down again. The water was clear and blue, and the top, which receded as he sank, looked like a shimmering sheet of glass. He kicked hard and shot to the surface again and, as he thrashed around, Sammy saw a rubber tube bobbing on top of the water. Desperate, he reached for it.

"Hold on with two hands and kick." Sammy turned his head and saw Adam swimming beside him. "C'mon, Sammy, you can do it. Kick hard."

He brushed hair out of his eyes, grabbed onto the tube, and followed Adam. When they reached the edge, Sammy let go of the tube, grasped the side of the pool, and rubbed water from his eyes. Then he looked up at Aunt Pearl. The hem of her white cotton dress was soggy with pool water. She had lost her sun hat and her hair fell around her face in a bird's nest of frizzy dark brown strands. Joshua was beside her, laughing his head off.

"Sorry, Aunt Pearl," Sammy pointed his thumb at Adam. "He's teaching me to swim."

"To drown, you mean," Joshua hooted.

Mrs. Weiss handed Aunt Pearl her hat and glared at Sammy. "Such a naughty boy! Scaring your aunt like that." She looked pointedly at Naomi, who was rocking the sleeping David in his pram. "When we bring relatives up and *treat them* for the summer, we don't expect them to give us trouble."

Naomi pinched her lips and shot Sammy a sympathetic gaze.

After the women and Joshua went back to the main house, Adam helped Sammy climb onto the deck.

"Next time, start in the shallow end." Adam smiled and patted Sammy's shoulder. "And try it without your shoes."

Mr. Liebman walked up to them. "Adam, you are supposed to be conducting a swimming lesson."

"Yes, Mr. Liebman." Adam walked to the shallow end of the pool. He blew his whistle. "Lesson time," he called, waving for the children to get into the water. "Tonight," he whispered, as Sammy joined him, "meet me at the lake after you finish cleaning up from dinner."

Adam was waiting for Sammy at the sandy strip that edged the lake. The sky was pink with the last of the day's sunshine.

"Tonight's the full moon. Ready to catch a ghost?" Adam pointed his chin at the Hermit's shack on the hill.

Sammy hesitated. He had promised his father that he wouldn't get into trouble this summer. He started to say as much to Adam, but stopped. *If we come out while everyone is asleep and get back before they wake up, they won't know we're gone*, he reasoned. *That way, I won't get into trouble. Will I?* He turned to Adam. "I'm ready."

They hadn't brought a light with them and the woods were dark. Adam led and Sammy tried to walk in his footsteps. A light mist curled through the treetops. Sammy could smell the rot of decaying leaves under his feet. As they reached the top, they stepped into a clearing and there was the Hermit's cabin.

"It's not as spooky as I thought it would be," Sammy whispered.

They crept closer. The cabin was dark, curtains drawn across the window facing them. Somewhere in the woods, an owl hooted.

"How are we going to look for clues if we can't see much?" asked Sammy.

But before Adam could reply, they heard something in the distance. Could it be hoof beats? But who would be riding a horse at this time of night? The sound grew closer and suddenly a horse and rider crashed out of the woods and galloped towards the cabin. Sammy jumped, grabbed Adam's hand, and pulled him behind the chicken coop. Breathing hard, he peered around the corner towards the cabin and squinted to make out the figure.

"Adam! The Hermit was right—it *is* a headless horseman!"

Adam peered around Sammy and gasped. The rider was dressed in black with a billowing cape, but where his head should've been, there was only empty space.

Suddenly the horse turned towards them and let out a high-pitched whinny. Sammy stumbled back.

"Time to go!" Adam quickly pulled Sammy up. The two fled into the woods, running as fast as they could, with the eerie sound of the horseman's laugh echoing behind them.

CHAPTER SEVEN

LIGHTS OUT

"Adam, did we really see a headless horseman last night or did I dream it?"

"It was real." Adam straightened the blanket on his bed and turned to Sammy.

"How are we supposed to fight a phantom?"

"I don't know, but we'll be ghosts if we don't get into the kitchen soon," Adam joked.

"We can't let that happen," Sammy laughed. "There's already one ghost causing trouble there. I don't think Mrs. Liebman can handle any more."

Uncle Milton came up to join the family until Sunday. That night at dinner, he was shocked to see Sammy waiting on tables.

"What's this? What's this? What's this?" he said as Sammy set a bowl of beet borscht in front of him.

"It's soup, Uncle Milton."

Aunt Pearl patted her husband's hand. "Sammy is helping out. To pay for his board."

"Does Ruben know about this?"

"My father thinks it's a good idea," Sammy interrupted. "He says I'm lucky to be spending the summer away from the city." This was only half true. Sammy's father thought Sammy was staying with Aunt Pearl, Leah, and Joshua in the main house, but Sammy was happy that he wasn't.

Uncle Milton seemed unconvinced but settled back in his chair and looked around the table. "So, is everybody happy, happy, happy?"

"What'd you say?" asked Molly as she pressed her ear horn against her ear.

"I asked if everyone was happy, happy, happy," Uncle Milton shouted.

"You don't have to shout! Goodness, I'm not deaf. We're all looking forward to the Fourth of July celebrations."

"Yes, indeed." Mr. Katzenblum adjusted his monocle and looked at Sammy. "Though I do hope your nephew can manage to stay alive until then, Doctor."

"What's this? Did something happen, Sammy?" asked Uncle Milton.

Sammy's face burned with shame. "It's nothing, Uncle Milton." *I* will *learn to swim this summer*, he silently vowed, *even if it kills me.*

After dinner, the guests went out on the porch to catch the evening breeze. Sammy sat on the steps with Adam and Shayna. By agreement, Adam and Sammy didn't discuss the incident of the previous night. Naomi joined them for a few minutes and then went upstairs to put David to bed. Sammy looked up at the still sunny sky. Suddenly Adam jumped to his feet.

"Look who's here. It's Moishe, the tummler!"

Sammy turned to see a short, wiry man dressed in baggy blue pants held up by wide blue suspenders, and a red-and-white striped shirt. He had a cheery face, with a prominent nose, dark eyes, and curly black hair under a white sailor's cap.

"Hello, friends." Moishe leaped onto the porch steps and pulled Molly to her feet. She laughed as he held her arm over her head and twirled her in a circle.

Molly's delight spread to the other guests. Soon

everyone was laughing and clapping as Moishe danced with the women and poked fun at the men.

"So, the good doctor is here," he said to Uncle Milton. He rubbed his back. "Oy, my back hurts. See?" He turned, jutting his rear end into Uncle Milton's face. "Such a pain! Tell me, doctor, what can you do for me?"

Uncle Milton took the fan from his wife's hand. "Nothing like a good swat to cure what ails you. Spank, spank, spank," he said, pretending to tap Moishe on the rear.

Moishe jumped forward. His mouth formed a wide *O*. Everyone laughed.

"Now it is time for a song." He spread his arms and began to sing.

Lomeer trinken a lekhayim!

(Let us drink a toast to life)

Tayere Sadie gezunt zolstu zany,

(Dear Sadie healthy should you be)

He pointed to Mrs. Weiss who clapped her hands and laughed.

Gees on dem bekher, dem bekher mit vayn.

(Fill up the goblet, the goblet with wine)

Bim bom bim bom bim bom bim bom

Bim bom bin bom bim bom bim bon.

As he sang, Sammy edged closer. He knew that song. It was one that his mother had often sung to Malka and him. Without thinking, Sammy joined in.

"Oh, we have a young entertainer here, do we?" Moishe motioned for Sammy to continue and they finished the song together.

"Bravo, bravo, bravo," clapped Uncle Milton.

Mrs. Liebman came running out on the porch. She looked around frantically until she spotted her husband, who was chatting with Uncle Milton.

"What's wrong?" Mr. Leibman jumped to his feet. "Has something happened?"

She clapped a hand to her forehead. "The light in the casino ceiling fell down. It missed me by this much." She pinched her thumb and forefinger together. "It's my *bubbie*. She is doing this. She is causing the trouble!"

"Come now, Rose." Mr. Liebman put an arm around her shoulders. "How could your grandmother cause trouble? She's dead."

"Why would your grandmother want to kill you?" asked Mr. Katzenblum.

"She always favoured my brother. She wants him to

have the hotel."

"I don't believe in ghosts," said Mrs. Weiss. "Someone is playing a trick on you."

"Please, don't worry. Everything's fine," Mr. Liebman announced to the guests. "The light's cord probably snapped. We'll fix it in no time."

Shayna took her mother's arm. "Come, Mama. Let's go inside. I'll make you a cup of tea."

After they left, Adam introduced Sammy to Moishe.

"You have a nice voice, Sammy," Moishe said. "Maybe you will sing with me sometime. Then he took off his hat and walked around the porch. After everyone had dropped in a coin or two, he bowed and went into the hotel.

"Hey, you should be a tummler too," Adam said as he and Sammy left the porch.

Sammy laughed. "My father wouldn't like that."

"You would make lots of money."

"Yeah, like Simba, the organ grinder's monkey." The organ grinder and Simba were a fixture on Orchard Street. Sammy had often stood with others watching Simba dart through the crowd, cap in hand, begging for money. "No." He shook his head. "I don't want to be a tummler."

As Adam and Sammy walked to their bungalow, Sammy thought about what had happened. "I don't think it was a ghost that shattered the light. It probably just came loose, like Mr. Liebman said."

"Or some unseen hand ripped it out of the ceiling and threw it down." Adam grinned. "Maybe it was Mrs. Liebman's grandmother or maybe it wasn't, but we do have spirits haunting the Catskills. And we've got to figure out how to catch one in particular."

CHAPTER EIGHT

THE HOUSE ON THE HILL

"Does Moishe stay here too?" Sammy asked while he and Adam were gathering eggs in the henhouse the following morning.

"Moishe?" Adam shook his head. "No, he lives at Mrs. Schwartz's bungalow colony just outside of Loch Sheldrake. He does odd jobs for her and people in town during the day, and on weekends and evenings, he goes around to the guesthouses to entertain."

"Let's go to the Hermit's house again tonight," Sammy said, as they stepped outside with their filled egg baskets.

"Okay," said Adam. "But we'll bring a flashlight this time. Got any ideas on what to do if the Horseman shows up?"

"Not exactly. But maybe we can figure out why he's

haunting the Hermit."

"Okay, but for now, we'd better get these eggs inside before your aunt and uncle start screaming for their breakfast."

At six o'clock, everyone gathered in the dining room for the *Shabbos* dinner. Mrs. Liebman lit the candles and the women recited the blessing. Then Uncle Milton made the *kiddush*, the blessing over the sweet wine that the Liebmans made from raisins.

"It is only for religious purposes," Mr. Liebman explained when Sammy asked about Prohibition, the law that forbid the sale or drinking of alcoholic beverages. "You are not allowed to have liquor, but a little wine for the kiddush, that they allow."

Mr. Liebman passed around the kiddush cup and everyone took a sip. Sammy puckered his lips. "I like the grape juice my father uses better," he whispered to Adam.

"Don't tell Mr. Liebman," he laughed.

Sammy and Adam helped the Liebmans serve the chicken soup with egg noodles, roast chicken, potato pudding, roasted carrots, and apple cake. After the guests were finished, the boys cleared the dishes, then sat at the round table in the kitchen with the Liebmans and ate their dinner. By the time they finished, it was nine o'clock and most of the guests had drifted off to their rooms or bungalows.

"So, you still want to go back to the Hermit's house?" Adam asked when he and Sammy emerged onto the porch.

The sky had darkened to a deep blue with wisps of mauve-tinted cloud. Sammy heard crickets chirping in the lilac bush at the bottom of the steps. A swing creaked in the corner of the porch and the sound of Shayna's voice and Leah's giggles drifted towards them. Sammy looked across the lawn to the copse of trees. Beyond it, the outline of a hill, round like a camel's hump, rose into the air.

Sammy looked over his shoulder. Aunt Pearl was rounding the corner and heading for the swing. She turned and caught his eye. Sammy grabbed Adam's arm.

"Let's go," he said. "Now!"

"Sammy," called Aunt Pearl. Sammy sighed and turned to face his aunt. "Your father sent a letter saying that he'll be arriving for the Fourth of July weekend."

"That's great, Aunt Pearl."

"He'll be bringing Martha with him, so I want you on your best behavior. No trouble—understand?"

Sammy understood all too well. *We'll have to put the ghost search on hold,* he thought.

"And one more thing." Aunt Pearl was warming up for her final decree. "No craziness in the dining room. You will act like a *mensch*. Do you know what is a *mensch?*"

"A good person," Sammy said in a tired voice.

"That's right." She placed her hand on his head. "Now, you should go to bed."

"Bed? It's only nine o'clock."

"Growing boys need their rest."

"I'm going, I'm going." Sammy motioned for Adam to follow him. "But she can't make me sleep," he whispered as they walked towards their bungalow.

"So, where were you Wednesday night?" Joshua leaned against Sammy and Adam's bungalow, his arms folded across his chest.

"What are *you* doing here?" Adam asked, unimpressed.

"We weren't anywhere that night," said Sammy defensively.

"Liar." Joshua unfolded his arms and stepped forward. "I was bored listening to Mama snore that night so I came out to play with you. But you weren't here." He circled Sammy.

"Go away, Joshua." Adam brushed past him and headed inside.

"You went up to the Hermit's place, didn't you?" Joshua screwed his face into an expression that told Sammy he was anxious to make trouble. "You *did* go there, didn't you?"

"So what if we did?" Sammy took a deep breath.

"So, if you did, *my* mother is going to tell *your* father and *you* are going to be in *big* trouble."

"And how is *your mother* going to find out?" Adam balled his fists and stepped towards Joshua.

Joshua grinned. "You're not going to hit me. Because if you do, I'll run into the house and scream." He put his hands on his hips and faced them. "But if you take me with you next time, I promise not to tell."

"It's scary up there," Adam said. "I don't think you're brave enough to come with us."

"I'm as brave as you are." Joshua puffed out his chest.

"Sure you are," Sammy snickered. "I remember how brave you were on Orchard Street when Herschel and his gang..."

"Shut up, Sammy." Joshua turned to Adam. "I'm as brave as *he* is." He flicked his thumb at Sammy. "Just try me."

Adam and Sammy exchanged glances. Sammy sighed. "Okay, next time we go you can come with us. Only promise me one thing," he said, as Joshua grinned in triumph.

"Sure, what?"

"If anything really scary happens, don't embarrass me by peeing in your pants."

CHAPTER NINE

ANOTHER SWIMMING LESSON

"So, are you ready to learn to swim?" Adam and Sammy were in their room. Sunday lunch was over and they had the afternoon free.

"I guess so." Sammy looked up at Adam. "Promise I won't drown."

"I promise. I'll be your lifeguard."

"I still don't have a proper swimming costume."

"You can borrow mine."

"But you're bigger than me."

"That's what safety pins are for."

Sammy sighed. "I guess I'm out of excuses."

"I guess you are." Adam tossed a swimsuit in Sammy's lap. "Put it on. I'll pin the straps for you and then we can go to the pool."

Sammy walked to the edge of the pool. Adam's bathing suit was two sizes too big and the pins made the top bunch up around his shoulders so it stood out like a tent. It was a hot day and the deck around the pool was crowded. Aunt Pearl was sitting at a table playing cards with three other women. They all wore big floppy hats to shield themselves from the sun. Joshua sat on a chair next to his mother but when he saw Sammy, he leapt to his feet and bounded over.

"Ychh. *What* are you wearing?" He poked a finger at Sammy's chest.

"Stop it!" Sammy backed away from Joshua, slipped, and fell into the water.

Splash! He was underwater, the oversize swimsuit billowing around him and pulling him down. He thrashed about with his arms and legs. It felt like forever until his feet touched bottom. Kicking as hard as he could, he pushed himself up towards the surface and managed to paddle to the side of the pool. Adam reached down and grasped his hand.

"One, two, three, up!" He pulled Sammy onto the deck and then hoisted him to his feet.

"Hey, look at Sammy." Joshua's voice hit Sammy like a slap.

"Sammy! Pull up your bathing suit!" Aunt Pearl said in a shocked voice.

Uh oh! Sammy looked down to where Adam's suit had puddled around his ankles.

"Cover up, right now!" Aunt Pearl handed him a towel. "First you jump into the pool when you can't swim. Then you come up naked. Oy!" She slapped her forehead. "I do your father one little favour and look what *tsoriss* it gets me." She poked Sammy's back. "March this minute to your room and *put on some clothes!*"

"Adam, I could kill you," Sammy said when they were alone in their room.

"I'm sorry." Adam covered his mouth so Sammy wouldn't see his grin.

"Stop laughing. It isn't funny." Sammy quickly dressed in short pants and a white shirt and then plopped onto the bed. *I was naked in front of Joshua and Aunt Pearl. As if things aren't bad enough. Now I have to listen to his teasing and her scolding.* "I'll never learn to swim," he moaned.

"Yes, you will. I have to go into town tomorrow to pick up groceries. Come with me and we'll buy you a bathing suit."

"I don't have any money."

"Maybe your aunt will lend you the money. After all," he said as Sammy started to protest, "she doesn't want you to swim naked again, does she?"

"No." Sammy started to laugh. "Did you see the look on her face? It was worth almost drowning. Next time let's get Joshua in the water and see what happens. I'll bet he can't swim either."

"I should loan you money? For what?"

"Papa will pay you back, I promise." Sammy hated pleading with his aunt but this was important. If he didn't get a swimsuit, he would never learn to swim.

"Pearl, the boy needs to learn to swim. We can't have him drowning, now can we? Can we? Can we? How would we explain that to Ruben?" Uncle Milton reached into his pocket and pulled out a roll of bills. "Here you are, Sammy," he said, peeling off two one dollar bills. "It will be our present, present, present to you."

Sammy swallowed. He hated taking the money, but the thought of wearing Adam's swimsuit again was even worse. "Thank you, Uncle Milton." He turned and fled from the room.

Joshua was waiting for him on the porch. "Boy, you sure looked stupid without your pants."

"Shut up, Joshua."

"And jumping into the deep end when you can't swim was really dumb."

"Not as dumb as you." Sammy clenched his fists. No one got under his skin like Joshua. *The Awful Joshua,* he reminded himself.

"Well, my mother didn't want you to come here with us. It was my father's idea."

"Hey! You want to come with us to the Hermit's house, don't you?"

Joshua nodded.

"Then stop acting like a jerk!" Sammy whirled around so fast that he almost tripped over his own feet. He stomped down the steps and stalked across the lawn to his bungalow. He was fuming as he entered the room. But he didn't stay angry for long because Adam was waiting for him.

"Moishe wants to see us. Actually, it's you he wants to see. About singing. C'mon." He grabbed Sammy's arm. "He's waiting on the porch."

CHAPTER TEN

IN THE SPOTLIGHT

"So, you're a singer, are you?" Moishe asked when they were settled on the porch. Sammy and Adam were sprawled on the steps while Moishe rocked back and forth on Mrs. Liebman's wicker chair.

"S-s-sort of." Sammy stammered.

"You've got a good voice, boychik. You did well that night—even brought down some lights," Moishe joked.

"Every time something goes wrong here, Mrs. Liebman swears that her dead grandmother did it," said Adam.

"Ah ha, the Pine Grove ghost strikes again." Moishe rubbed his hands together.

"Moishe, I've been hearing ghost stories since I was a baby." Adam shook his head. "But that's all they are. Stories!"

"But, Adam, we did see…"

"We did not see anything!" Adam looked Sammy in the eye. "We heard a noise. In the bushes. An animal. That's all. Right?"

"Right," Sammy said as Mrs. Liebman bustled over to them.

"There you are, Mr. Tummler. So, what are you waiting for? Our guests are ready."

"Yes, yes, Mrs. Liebman." Moishe rose to his feet. "Come on, Sammy. Time to put on a show."

"Me?"

"Yes, you. You think I'm talking to the Statue of Liberty?"

Sammy stood, brushed off the seat of his pants and followed Moishe. As he reached the door, he looked back. "See you later, Adam?"

"You bet." Adam held up his hand.

The minute they entered the parlor, Moishe went into his act. Jumping up and down he clapped his hands and began to sing.

Toot, toot, Tootsie, goodbye.
Toot, toot, Tootsie, don't cry.

The choo choo train that takes me

Away from you, no words can tell how sad it makes me...

"Just like Eddie Cantor," Mrs. Liebman sighed.

"Who's Eddie Cantor?" Adam asked.

"The best entertainer in the world," said Aunt Pearl.

"What did you say?" Molly pressed the silver horn against her ear.

"I said that Eddie Cantor is the best entertainer in the world!" Aunt Pearl shouted.

"You don't have to scream," screamed Molly. "I'm not deaf, you know. Eddie Cantor is the king of vaudeville."

Sammy knew about vaudeville. He had even been to a show in the Palace Theatre. He'd loved all the acts: a ventriloquist and his dummy, a lady singer, and four men who called themselves a "barbershop quartet." When he asked if they worked in a real barbershop, Aunt Tsippi had explained that being a barbershop quartet meant they sang in a four-part harmony.

Moishe finished his song and grabbed Sammy's hand. He pulled him over to the piano, sat on the stool, and pounded the keys. "Sing, Sammy, sing!"

"Sing what?" Sammy turned to him.

"Sing 'My Yiddishe Momme'," said Mrs. Liebman.

"I know that song." Sammy pulled himself up to his full height and sang.

The haunting melody filled the casino as Sammy's voice rose and waltzed through the heartfelt song.

"Oy, that song always makes me cry." Mrs. Liebman pulled a lace handkerchief from her pocket and dabbed at her eyes. "Such a beautiful voice. *Pooh, pooh, pooh.*"

As he finished the song, Sammy lifted his hands, palms up, and put tears into his voice. The audience exploded with applause.

"Thank you, thank you," he bowed.

"More! More!" they chanted. Shayna took over the piano as Moishe and Sammy sang more songs throughout the night. It was exhilarating and nerve-wracking, but Sammy never felt more like he belonged.

CHAPTER ELEVEN

THE HERMIT'S HOUSE

The following night, the boys went back to the Hermit's house. Only this time Joshua joined them.

"How did you sneak away from your mother?" Sammy asked Joshua as they started towards the hill.

"I told her that we were helping Mrs. Liebman."

"I thought she doesn't want you to work."

"I said *helping* her, not working for her."

Adam and Sammy exchanged looks. "He's *your* cousin."

"Don't I know it," Sammy muttered.

They entered the woods, silently made their way to the road, and then climbed up the hill. The sky was a blanket of clouds and the air was heavy with moisture. Thunder rumbled in the distance. "Turn on the flashlight," Sammy said as he tripped over a rock.

"And give ourselves away? We don't want him to know that we're up here."

"He'll know if he finds our broken bodies in the morning."

They finished the rest of the climb in silence. As they neared the top of the hill, Sammy saw a faint light coming from the Hermit's cabin.

"What are we going to do when we get there?" Joshua asked.

"Investigate." Adam said.

"Investigate what?"

"The Headless Horseman," answered Sammy.

"The what? The legend Mr. Klein was joking about?"

Sammy and Adam looked at each other. "No, he's pretty real."

"You guys saw him?"

"Quiet!" hissed Adam. Crouching low, he walked to the cabin's window. "Stay down," Adam ordered. He pulled himself up just enough to see over the sill.

"What's he doing?" Sammy lifted his head and peered inside. The Hermit was bending over a potbelly stove, feeding it twigs. The only light came from the stove and a small oil lamp in the middle of a table. The Hermit was wearing the same coveralls and plaid shirt he had been in when they'd met him at Mr. Klein's store. His head was bowed and Sammy saw the ropey muscles in the back of his neck.

"Uh oh." Adam looked up as thunder rumbled across the sky, followed by the sharp crack of a lightning bolt. As if someone had overturned a full bucket, rain pelted down. The boys scrambled to find shelter.

"Get under the trees!" Sammy shouted.

"Are you crazy? That's the last place you want to be in a thunderstorm." Adam gave Sammy an amused look. "You really are a city boy."

"I lived in the country in Poland."

"Don't they have thunderstorms in Poland?"

"Adam…" Sammy looked up as a dark form loomed over his friend.

"You need to loosen up, Sammy. Stop being afraid of your own shadow," taunted Joshua.

"GUYS!"

"Gotcha!" A hand reached out, grabbed Adam's shoulder, and spun him around.

Sammy felt a vise-like grip on his arm. He looked up. He was staring into the angry eyes of the Hermit.

"Here, dry yourselves off before you catch pneumonia." The Hermit handed each of them a towel. Then he pointed to a sofa. "Sit!" he ordered.

Sammy plopped onto one end. Adam sat on the other with Joshua in the middle. Sammy looked around the room as he dried off. It was cozier than he'd expected. A braided rug was topped by what looked like a hand carved wooden table and four cane-back chairs. The potbelly cast iron stove squatted in the far corner near a metal sink. A rocking chair was in front of the stove. Next to it, a round table held a Bible and a bowl of apples.

Sammy looked up. The Hermit towered over them.

"Okay. I'm waiting for an explanation."

Sammy squirmed. Next to him, Adam slouched, elbows on knees.

"Well?" The Hermit tapped his foot.

"We're trying to help you," Sammy blurted out.

"Help *me*?"

"Yeah."

"That's right." Adam sat up straight. "We know about the Horseman."

The Hermit's expression turned grim. His brow creased, his eyes narrowed, and his lips stretched tight across his teeth. For a minute, it looked as if he was going to hit them. Then he shook himself, took a deep breath, and walked to the window.

"Y'all have quite the imagination. The storm has stopped. Time you boys went back to where you belong." He opened the door and motioned for them to move. "Go! Scat! And don't come back!"

As they moved to the door, the sound of a whip cracked the air, followed by a shrill whinny. They stumbled outside just in time to see a horseman gallop by at full speed, turn down the hill, and disappear into the woods.

"It's him!" Sammy shouted.

"Who?" asked Joshua.

"The chickens are loose!" Adam pointed to the chicken coop. The gate was open and the chickens were squawking their heads off, feathers flying as they ran in circles around the yard.

"Not again. Don't just stand there," the Hermit ordered. "Help me get them back in the coop."

Sammy ran one way and Adam the other. "Shoo, shoo," Sammy yelled, guiding them back towards the open gate. "You're going the wrong way." He picked up a hen and put her in the coop.

"Do you know why he's haunting you?" Sammy asked when all the chickens had been gathered up. "You told Mr. Klein that this kind of thing has happened before."

The Hermit looked down at the boys. "You listen here and you listen good. There are no such things as ghosts." He turned, walked into his house, and slammed the door.

Sammy walked over to the chicken coop and tested the door to make sure it was securely bolted. As he walked to the gate, he stopped and stared at the post. "Adam, look. Blood."

"It's probably chicken blood," Joshua said.

"No. It's too high." Sammy pointed to a spot above his shoulder. "It's not chicken blood."

"It could be the Hermit's," Adam said.

"It's fresh. And the Hermit didn't look hurt." Sammy looked at the woods. "It could be the Headless Horseman's. And if it is, that proves he's not a ghost, because ghosts don't bleed. He's a real person who can be caught."

CHAPTER TWELVE

WHO IS THE HERMIT?

"Moishe, what do you know about the Hermit?" Lunch was over. The tables were cleared and the guests were either in their rooms sleeping off the heat of the day or at the pool. Moishe and Sammy had the parlor to themselves. Moishe was picking out tunes on the piano while Sammy stared out the window.

"Sammy, the Fourth of July is on Tuesday. Don't bother me about the Hermit. Besides, why are you so interested in him all of a sudden?"

"I...I think he's in danger," Sammy blurted out.

"Danger? From what?"

"I think someone's trying to hurt him."

"You know what I think? I think you have a good imagination."

"I'm not imagining it." Sammy sat beside Moishe on the piano bench. He swallowed hard. "Why is someone terrorizing the Hermit? And why does he live up there all alone, away from everyone?"

"Ah, Sammy. I don't know anything about someone terrorizing him, but he has his reasons for keeping to himself. The man you call the Hermit is named Ezekiel Parker—Zeke for short. He was born on a plantation in the state of Georgia. In school, you learned about the Civil War?"

Sammy nodded. "Uh huh."

"Zeke hated being a slave, so when the war started, he escaped and made his way north. To earn money, he worked on farms. When he got here, he worked for Ebenezer Thackeray, and when the old man died, he left the cabin and his property to Zeke."

"If the Hermit was born a slave, he must be really old."

"Well, I guess he's a little over seventy, but he's still strong as a bull."

"Why does he live up there alone?"

"He had a wife once, but she died. We don't see much of him because, well, you see…" Moishe stared off into the distance. "How do I put this? Zeke is black. Black people and white people don't mix."

"Why not?"

Moishe shrugged. "People can be very stupid and mean. Tell me, in Poland, you were friends with your Christian neighbours?"

"No." Sammy shook his head. "They didn't like Jews, so we kept to ourselves. Especially at Easter." He shuddered at the memory of soldiers attacking Jewish homes because of lies about Jews using the blood of Christian babies to bake matzo. "That's why Papa brought us to America."

"Well, even in America people aren't always good." Moishe placed his hands on the piano keys and nodded at Sammy. "Okay, *Samelech*, what song will we practice first?"

After Moishe left, Sammy thought about what he'd said. In Sammy's neighbourhood in New York, the Jewish kids hung out together while the Italians had their own gang and the Irish kids had theirs. The first time Sammy had met his neighbour, Luigi, he said, "Orchard Street is *my territory*." Sammy didn't know what he meant but he soon found out. Sometimes fights broke out between the gangs when one or the other claimed a street corner or a playground as their own. Sammy thought about the guests at the hotel. *Everyone here is Jewish. Maybe Moishe is right. People just like being with their own kind.* Was that why someone was terrorizing the Hermit? Because he wasn't Jewish? Or because he was black? Or was there a deeper, more sinister reason?

CHAPTER THIRTEEN

NEW GUESTS ARRIVE

S ammy had to put thoughts of the Hermit and the Horseman aside as he and Adam plunged into the task of preparing for the July Fourth holiday. The dining room had to be arranged with several large round tables added to hold the extra guests who had arrived and others— including Sammy's father and new stepmother—who were arriving today. He cringed at the thought. *I'm glad Papa has found someone to be with because he was lonely. But what if she wants me to call her Mama? I don't think I can do that.*

"Hey, Sammy, hurry up. It's almost two o'clock and we have to meet the train."

"Okay." Sammy buttoned his shirt, ran his fingers through his hair, and followed Adam outside. Hot humid air engulfed them. Staying in the country was a relief from the torture of a New York summer, but it was still hot. Sammy glanced longingly at the swimming pool as he crossed the yard.

"A couple more lessons and you'll be swimming like a fish," Adam assured him.

"I don't want to be a fish. I just want to cool off." Sammy wiped sweat off his forehead. "What happens up here on the Fourth of July?"

"For one thing, the hotel is full, so it means a lot more work for us. C'mon." He headed for the wagon. "We can't miss the train."

The station platform was crowded when the train chugged to a stop. The scene was much the same as it had been when Sammy had arrived a week earlier. Hawkers stood atop their wagons trying to attract customers.

"Come to our farm. Only fifteen dollars for a bungalow and three meals a day," called a bearded man in a farmer's coveralls.

"The day we arrived staying at his farm was only twelve dollars," Sammy said.

"They raise the prices for holidays." Adam pointed to a man in a dark suit helping a woman wearing a wide-brimmed white hat down from the train. "Are those your parents?"

"My father—not my parents."

"Sorry." Adam shuffled his feet. "What do you call her?"

"I don't know." Sammy waved. "Papa!" he hollered.

The man turned, saw Sammy, and waved back. A moment later, Sammy was enveloped in a smothering hug. He disentangled himself and looked up into his stepmother's face.

"Sammy, my son." She pulled a white lace handkerchief from her pocket. "So silly of me to cry." She dabbed at her eyes. "I am just so happy to be here."

Sammy looked at Adam and rolled his eyes.

"Please," she said, pinching Sammy's cheek, "call me Mama."

"I think it's a bit early for that," his father gently chided her.

"Then what will he call me?" Her blue eyes opened wide.

"How about *Tanta*," Sammy said, using the Yiddish word for aunt.

"Tanta Martha," his father nodded. "Is that all right

with you?" he asked his wife.

Before she could answer, Adam stepped between them. "Welcome, Mr. and Mrs. Levin. Let me help you." He lifted their valise, hefted it into the back of the wagon, and motioned for them to get in. "Please..." He looked at the sky. The sun told him it was getting late. "We'd better get going. We don't want to miss dinner."

Sammy climbed up next to Adam, who lifted the reins. Simon whinnied, tossed his head, and bolted forward.

It's going to be a long week, Sammy thought as they rode back to the hotel in a swirl of dust churned up by the wagon's wheels. Behind him, Tanta Martha held onto her hat with one hand and covered her nose and mouth with the other. Sammy's father sat straight and tall beside her. They rode the rest of the way in silence.

"My son is what?" Papa's face was beet red as he glared at Aunt Pearl.

"He is helping out the Liebmans. Such a good boy." She patted Sammy's arm and he cringed.

"You brought him here to be hired help? Without telling me?" He looked as if he would explode.

Sammy stepped in. "It's all right, Papa. I like it. I get

to stay in the bungalow with Adam. And the Liebmans are really nice." *And,* he thought, *I don't have to be with Joshua.*

"That's not the point," his father fumed.

"Ruben." Tanta Martha took his arm, trying to diffuse the situation. "Let's go to our room and clean up."

"Yes, Papa. That's a good idea." Sammy lifted their bag and headed for the stairs.

"Give me that." His father snatched the bag from his hands. "You are not my servant! As for you," he turned to Pearl, "you are…"

"Ruben, darling, if it weren't for me, your precious Sammy would be sweltering in the city and running around with his gang. At least up here he won't get into trouble. You should thank me." And with that, she marched out to the porch, her ample behind swaying as she walked.

After dinner everyone gathered in the parlor for the night's entertainment. Tonight Moishe was wearing baggy pants with bright red suspenders, a red-and-white checked shirt, and a black hat with an enormous red flower stuck in the band. The guests were seated on sofas and chairs arranged in a circle.

"And now, for my partner in song…let's have a big

hand for Sammy Levin! Sammy, where are you?" Moishe looked around the room. Sammy waved to him from the corner where he'd been slouching, hoping he wouldn't be seen. With a sigh, Sammy stepped forward and joined him.

Everyone clapped—except Sammy's father, who was giving him a very strange look. Sammy couldn't tell if he was proud, embarrassed, or angry. Sammy looked back at him and grinned sheepishly.

Moishe went into his act and together they sang "Toot Toot Tootsie Goodbye," and then Sammy sang "My Yiddishe Mama." Papa looked stunned; Tanta Martha dabbed her eyes with a lace handkerchief. Then, before Moishe could ask him to sing another number, Sammy bowed to the audience and left the room.

CHAPTER FOURTEEN

SAMMY, THE TUMMLER

July fourth dawned clear and hot. The hotel was full and all the bungalows were occupied. There were twenty adults and nine children, including Leah. At breakfast, everyone was in a good mood. Even Aunt Pearl smiled as Sammy set a plate of eggs and onions in front of her. "You are learning to be a good waiter." She turned to Sammy's father. "You will see. He will come back to the city a changed boy."

Mr. Levin shook his head. "Pearl, you meddle too much."

"Meddle, *shmeddle*. I know what's good for a boy like your Sammy." She lowered her voice. "He won't get into trouble with the police up here."

"Police? He was in trouble with the police?" Tanta Martha asked.

"Nothing you need worry about." Papa patted her hand. "Our Sammy here is a good boy." Turning, he gave Sammy a stern look. "Aren't you, Sammy?"

"Yes, Papa." He gave his stepmother a defiant look. "It was only once and I was helping some friends stay *out* of trouble."

"Oh, well that's good then, Sammy. Your friends are lucky to have you." She smiled.

"Sure," he replied sullenly.

Mrs. Liebman came up to them. "Sammy, a word, please?"

"Yes, Mrs. Liebman." *What have I done? Did I put out the wrong dishes or ruin a tablecloth?*

"Your stepmother, she is a nice woman. She only wants to be good to you."

"I don't need her. I can take care of myself."

"Have you thought that maybe *she* needs someone to care for? Don't be so fast to throw a person away." She patted him on the shoulder.

"So, I hear you're going after a horseman," Shayna whispered as she and Sammy finished clearing the dishes.

"Who told you that?"

"Adam."

Adam! Sammy would have to talk to him about this later. "Yeah, we are. But I promised my father I'd stay out of trouble this summer. Promise not to tell anyone about our plans?"

"My lips are sealed. But if you boys ever need help, you know where to find me. I'm an excellent investigator, you know." Shayna smiled and headed into the kitchen.

Sammy was kept busy for the rest of the day. There were the breakfast dishes to clean and then the tables to set for lunch. It seemed that the only thing the hotel's guests were really interested in was food. "Everyone eats as if they are starving," he said to Adam as they placed dishes, knives, and forks at each place.

"That's because they pay the same whether they eat or not. They want to get their money's worth. Watch Molly. She always takes more than she can eat, then wraps the leftovers in her napkin and takes it to her room."

Sammy understood Molly. She too came from Europe where food had been scarce. Like him, she remembered being hungry.

They finished setting the tables, and then walked back

to the bungalow.

"Why'd you tell Shayna about the horseman?" asked Sammy.

Adam flushed. "Sorry, it kind of slipped out."

"Can we trust her?"

"Absolutely! I've worked with her for a few summers now and she's kept all my secrets."

"Sounds like you guys are pretty close," teased Sammy.

"We're *friends*, Sammy." The tips of Adam's ears were pink as he quickly shifted topics. "Are you going to do your act today?"

Sammy grimaced. Ever since his disaster at the pool, it had become a daily routine for him to jump into the water fully clothed and for Adam to fish him out. For some reason, the guests found this hilarious. Sammy held up the new bathing suit from their last trip into town. "At least my bathing costume won't fall off like the one you loaned me."

"They'd like it even better if it did."

"I don't think Papa would."

"He'll realize that it's just an act. C'mon, Sammy. Admit it. You're a born tummler."

A born tummler; a clown. In Poland, during the war, Sammy had gone door to door and sung for scraps of bread.

In New York, he'd sung to get his stickball back from Mr. Gresham after it had crashed into his pushcart. *And now I'm entertaining a bunch of bored women like my Aunt Pearl.* Yet, he had to admit that he found being an entertainer appealing. It was fun to make people smile; even more fun to make them laugh. "Okay, Adam," he said as they reached the pool. "Let's get this over with."

A few minutes later, wearing their bathing costumes underneath shorts, shirts, and wide-brimmed straw hats called boaters, they walked onto the pool deck. Aunt Pearl was sitting at a table with Tanta Martha and Molly, who was dealing cards. Sammy's father and Uncle Milton sat on chairs behind them. Papa looked stiff and uncomfortable in a starched white shirt and black pants. Uncle Milton wore a short-sleeved blue shirt open at the neck, and white pants. His face was splotched and red from sunburn. He looked up at Sammy, shielding his eyes.

"Like that you're dressed for the pool? Didn't I give you money for a bathing costume? Didn't I? Didn't I? Didn't I?"

Sammy didn't answer.

"Okay, Sammy. Showtime," Adam whispered in Sammy's ear. Then he strutted to the deep end of the pool and jumped in. Sammy followed him, shouting as he landed in the water. As he went under, he slapped the surface of the water and breathed out bubbles. Adam grabbed the back of Sammy's shirt and yanked him up. As he gasped for air, he heard screams. *Aunt Pearl and Tanta Martha.* The thought made him laugh and he breathed in water and started coughing.

"Pretend you're drowning," Adam instructed.

I won't have to pretend, Sammy thought as he thrashed about, kicking, flailing his arms, and gasping for breath. These past two weeks, Adam had taught him to stay afloat, and he was becoming a decent swimmer, but his waterlogged clothes were dragging him down. *I can't believe that this is what people want to see,* Sammy thought as he sank under the water again. Adam grasped Sammy and clutched him to his chest, paddled to the shallow end, and deposited him. Sammy threw his arms into the air and jumped up and down, retrieved his hat as it floated towards him, clamped it onto his wet hair, and bowed to scattered applause. Then he looked up into the shocked face of his father.

"Hi, Papa," Sammy grinned sheepishly. He hoisted himself onto the deck and stood, water streaming into puddles at his feet. "It's an act, Papa."

"From such an act you can drown." Sammy's father glared at him.

"You shouldn't scare your father like that," Tanta Martha scolded.

"That's between me and my father," Sammy snapped.

"Sammy!" Papa glared at him. "You talk to your mother with respect."

"She's not my mother!"

"She is my wife and you will respect her."

"But I don't have to like her," Sammy muttered under his breath.

"What was that?" Papa's voice was a growl.

"Nothing." Sammy turned to Tanta Martha. "I'm sorry. I didn't mean to be rude."

"It's all right," she sniffed.

Were those tears she was blinking back? Sammy was suddenly ashamed. "I really am sorry." He turned back to his father. "I didn't almost drown. I can swim," he half-lied.

"Since when?"

"Last week." Sammy pointed to Adam. "He taught me."

His father looked from Adam to Sammy and back

again. "*Meshugoyem.* Crazy." Shaking his head, he returned to his chair.

"Uh oh. Here she comes." Sammy stepped backwards as Aunt Pearl charged up.

"Again with the funnies? I almost had a heart attack."

"You see, Sammy's a tummler and that's what tummlers do," said Adam. "They make people laugh."

Aunt Pearl folded her arms across her chest. "I am *not* laughing."

"I didn't laugh," said Joshua.

"You don't know how to laugh," Sammy retorted.

"Almost drowning you think is funny?" Aunt Pearl sighed loudly. "Your mother, may she rest in peace, is turning in her grave."

"Don't talk about my mother!" Sammy shouted and stalked off to his bungalow.

Adam came in a few minutes later as Sammy finished changing.

"Hey, are you okay?" he asked gently, placing his towel on a chair and then sitting on it.

"Yeah." Sammy sniffed, trying to hide his unshed tears.

"You don't have to tell me if you don't want to, but what

happened to your mother?"

Sammy took a shaky breath. "Papa left for America when I was five. He was going to find work and then bring us to New York, but the war started and we couldn't get out of the country. It was terrible—everyone was fighting, there wasn't enough food, and lots of people were getting sick with the flu. I remember Mama, so sick she couldn't get out of bed. And my sister, Malka, taking care of her while I went through the village begging for food. Soldiers on horseback thundered down the main road of our village as we hid in haystacks."

"It sounds awful. I can't believe you survived that."

"Not all of us did. We tried so hard to take care of her, but Mama died and Malka and I were alone."

"You're not alone anymore," said Adam. He put his hand on Sammy's shoulder. "You've got me. And even if they are a pain, you've got your family, too."

Sammy gave him a half-smile. "That's true." He thought of how lucky he was to have his friends and family. *I can't imagine being all by myself with no one.* He paused. "And that's why we need to help the Hermit. He doesn't have a family to stick up for him. We need to stop the Horseman."

As evening approached, a sense of excitement built among the guests. Even Mr. Klein and some of the local residents came for the festivities. Celebrating the Fourth of July made them feel like real Americans. After dinner, everyone gathered on the lawn. Some people sat on chairs that had been set in a horseshoe; others spread blankets and sat on the grass. The children ran back and forth between the guests, waving American flags. A small stage had been set up in front of the porch. At seven o'clock, Adam stepped up and shouted for everyone to pay attention. The guests ignored him, continuing to laugh and joke, so Adam picked up a megaphone and repeated the command. "Ladies and gentlemen, do *we* have a show for *you!*"

"*Do* you have a show for *us?*" shouted a man in the audience.

"We sure do." Adam waved a hand and Moishe danced onto the stage. He immediately went into his act, telling jokes, teasing the women, and poking fun at the men. "Hey, Sammy," he called. "Get up on the stage. Ladies and gents, we are now going to sing a real Fourth of July song for you."

Yankee Doodle went to town riding on a pony,
stuck a feather in his hat and called it macaroni.
Yankee Doodle keep it up; Yankee Doodle dandy...

At first, Sammy felt shy, but as Moishe pranced around the stage, he became bolder and followed him. Together, they moved into the audience. "Sing, everybody sing," Moishe commanded and the audience joined in.

Yankee Doodle went to town riding on a pony,
stuck a feather in his hat and called it macaroni.

As Sammy performed, he felt energized. It was a beautiful night with soft, warm air. Lanterns hanging in the trees cast a glow over the audience. Everyone was having a good time. Even Aunt Pearl had lost her sour expression. Leah sat beside her, looking sweet in a pink cotton dress with a white sash. Uncle Milton clapped along to the music—three claps, a pause, then three more claps. *Just like he talks,* Sammy thought. On impulse, he pulled Leah to her feet and twirled her around and around until the faces of the audience became a blur.

Just then, a high-pitched whinny cracked the air like a clap of thunder. A black stallion ridden by a cloaked figure charged across the back of the lawn. Sammy's blood chilled.

The horse stopped and the rider turned to the crowd. Thinking it was part of the entertainment, everyone applauded. The rider cracked his whip and the horse turned and galloped away.

Sammy's head was spinning. *Why was the rider here? What did he want? And most important, who was he?* "Adam!" Sammy called as his friend ran over. "Did you see that?"

"Unless we're all dreaming, yes, I saw that. What the heck is going on?"

"I don't know, but this can't be good."

Joshua rushed over. "That was great! Where'd you get the horse and who was riding it?" Joshua hopped from one foot to the other. "C'mon, Sammy, tell me."

"Joshua, stop being an idiot," Sammy snapped. "I didn't set this up!" But before Sammy could explain, Moishe pulled him back into the spotlight for their final song.

CHAPTER FIFTEEN

THE ICHABODS

After the show, the boys gathered in Sammy and Adam's bungalow.

"Actually, there *is* an upside to the Horseman coming to the hotel," said Adam. "The lighting is way better here than it is up on that hill—and when the Horseman stopped, I could see that his horse has a white scar along its right shoulder."

"That's great!" said Sammy. "All we have to do now is find a horse with that same marking and it'll lead us to the Horseman!"

"Sammy, this is the countryside. Lots of people have horses and we can't go through all of them," countered Adam. After seeing Sammy's face fall, he added, "But that scar is a good clue."

"That's still not a lot to go on…"

"You're not helping, Joshua." Adam threw him a look.

"Okay, let's just think about this. Who would have a reason to do this to the Hermit?" Sammy asked, thinking out loud. "Does he have any enemies?"

Adam snorted. "The Hermit isn't the friendliest guy, but I wouldn't say he has enemies. He's up there all by himself, remember? I mean, the only people near him are us on this side of the hill and…wait!"

"The mountain men!" all three chorused.

"That's right! That day at the store!" Sammy remembered. "We've got to find them and investigate."

"Are you crazy? That man was terrifying," Joshua protested.

"Scared?" Adam teased.

"I didn't say that," Joshua huffed.

"*I'm* not," came a voice at the door. "We can solve this together."

The boys all turned and stared at Shayna who had come inside without their noticing.

"*We?*" Sammy sputtered.

"Yes, WE." Shayna sank to the floor and leaned against the cot. Even in the darkened bungalow, Sammy could see the wicked gleam in her eyes. "Girls make great sleuths."

"Yeah right," Joshua scoffed. "Name one."

Shayna ignored him. "What's the legend say about the Headless Horseman, anyway?"

"Let's see…" Adam took a book off the shelf over his bed. "*The Legend of Sleepy Hollow.* It's about a schoolteacher named Ichabod Crane who was spooked by a Headless Horseman. Here, listen." He sat on his cot and began to read. "'The dominant spirit that haunts this enchanted region is the apparition of a figure on horseback without a head. It is said to be the ghost of a Hessian trooper, whose head was carried away by a cannonball in some nameless battle during the Revolutionary War…' Then it goes on to say, 'The specter is known, at all the country firesides, by the name of the Headless Horseman of Sleepy Hollow.' Ichabod wanted to marry the daughter of a rich farmer. Her name was Katrina Van Tassel. But she had another guy after her. In the story, the guy's name was Brom Van Brunt, and he was a big, strong bully. Ichabod was tall and stringy and kind of a coward."

Sammy snapped his fingers. "I get it. Brom Van Brunt dressed up like this horseman in the legend and scared Ichabod away."

"And our Headless Horseman is trying to do the same thing to the Hermit," said Joshua.

"If he's after the Hermit, why did he come to the hotel?" Shayna asked.

"That's a good question," said Sammy.

"Maybe he thought the Hermit was here," said Adam. "Or he has another motive. Any ideas?"

"Hmm. We should check out the suspects first. If the mountain men are behind this, we have to get proof," Shayna spoke as the boys nodded. "And if we are going to work together, we need a name."

"Who said we're working together?" Joshua protested.

"And why not?" Shayna huffed, hands on hips, glaring at him. When Joshua didn't answer, she continued. "So, what do we call ourselves?"

"'The Avengers'?" said Joshua.

Everyone stared at him.

"That's what we're doing, isn't it? Avenging the Hermit?"

"First we have to find out what we're avenging," said Adam. "How about 'The Pine Grove Detectives'?"

"Too boring," said Shayna. "'The Fearsome Four'. There's four of us and we're going to be fearsome. Aren't we?"

Adam turned to Sammy. "You haven't said anything."

"Do we really need a name?"

"Yes!" the others chorused.

Sammy rested his chin in his hands and closed his eyes. After a minute he looked up. "How about 'The Ichabods'? You know, after Ichabod Crane?"

"Brilliant." Shayna took a pad of paper and a pencil from her skirt pocket. "The Ichabods," she wrote.

There was a knock at the door.

"Joshua, are you in there? Do you know what time it is?"

"Yes, Mama." He gave a sheepish grin. "She found me. I gotta go."

After he left, Shayna stood and straightened her skirt. "Tomorrow, The Ichabods, begin." She clapped a hand on each of their shoulders. "Good night, partners."

Sammy looked at Adam and shook his head. "I guess we have a gang."

"I guess we do. Hey, Sammy, is this anything like your gang in New York?"

My gang in New York. Sammy thought of Herschel and Tommy and the other guys. They had started out bullying him and then became his friends. "It's the same, but different," he answered. "We didn't have a girl in our gang on Orchard Street. And we were up against bullies our own age."

"A bully is a bully," Adam declared.

Sammy nodded. He could hardly wait to see what the next few days would bring.

CHAPTER SIXTEEN

BEWARE THE MOUNTAIN MEN

"That was quite a show, show, show, you put on last night, Sammy." Uncle Milton slapped Sammy's back so hard he almost dropped the plate of cheese blintzes he was holding. "Headless Horseman! Where did you get such a crazy, crazy, crazy idea?"

"From Washington Irving," he muttered. He had decided it was better to take credit for the incident rather than to try to explain it away. He set the plate down in front of his uncle.

"Is Mr. Irving staying here?" asked Mrs. Weiss.

"No. He's dead."

"Poor man," she sniffed.

"If he's dead, how can he give you ideas?" asked Molly.

"He was a writer. He wrote stories," Sammy explained.

"He snores?" Molly gave him a puzzled look and put her horn to her ear.

"No, he wrote *stories*," Sammy raised his voice.

"I keep telling you not to shout!" she shouted. "I'm not deaf."

"Sorry. I forgot." Sammy turned and walked back to the kitchen. Adam was unloading a tray of dirty dishes into the sink. "Adam, everyone thinks we staged that Headless Horseman stunt."

"Let them."

"They'll want us to do it again. Like they want us to jump in the pool in our clothes every day."

"That's life in the Catskills." Adam grinned.

"Oy, boychik, what a show you gave us!" Mrs. Liebman pinched Sammy's cheek.

"Ah, yes, Mrs. Liebman…only the best entertainment for your guests."

She laughed. "Such a joker. At first, I thought maybe it was Bubbie Bluma but then I said to myself, no, it couldn't be. How could a woman her age learn to ride a horse?"

"Uh, yes. That makes sense. Sort of." Sammy looked at Adam. He was trying not to laugh.

"So," Mrs. Liebman changed the subject. "What are

you going to do tonight?"

"Tonight?"

"Our guests aren't leaving yet. So, again we need to entertain them."

Adam looked at Sammy and winked. "We'll think of something, won't we *boychik*?"

"Of course we will." Sammy looked out the kitchen window. It was another hot, sunny day. His stepmother, Aunt Pearl, and Molly were playing gin rummy at one end of the porch while the men were playing a card game called pinochle at the other end. Naomi was on the lawn, watching Esther and a small girl play catch while baby David slept in his pram.

Mrs. Weiss came into the kitchen and stormed up to Mrs. Liebman. "What kind of hotel is this?" she fumed. "I bring my family here for a restful vacation and we have headless men riding wild horses. We could all be trampled."

Mrs. Liebman stared at Mrs. Weiss. "It was a joke. Part of the entertainment."

"Some entertainment! More jokes like that and I will leave and want my money back." She turned and marched out of the kitchen.

Mrs. Liebman looked at Sammy. "Next time, Sammy,

no horses. Okay?"

"Rose, what's all the commotion?" Mr. Liebman came into the kitchen and went to his wife's side.

"It is nothing." She went back to the counter and started kneading the dough.

Sammy turned to Mr. Liebman. "Mrs. Weiss threatened to leave because of the horseman." He thought for a minute. "Mr. Liebman, what do you know about the mountain men?"

"The mountain men? You stay away from them." Mr. Liebman shook a meaty finger in Sammy's face. "Those men are trouble."

"Trouble, *shmubble*. You'll know trouble if we don't get the tables set before the guests come in for lunch," said Mrs. Liebman.

"Better listen to her, Sammy. You think the mountain men are fierce? They have nothing on my wife!" Mr. Liebman laughed and walked into the dining room.

Mrs. Liebman turned to Adam. "I need more flour. And coffee. You and Sammy go into town."

CHAPTER SEVENTEEN

ANOTHER TRIP TO TOWN

The bell over the door jangled as the boys entered the store. Mr. Klein turned from the shelf he had been rearranging and greeted them with a smile. "Hello, young men. Great show last night! What can I do for you today?"

Adam pulled a list from his pocket. "Mrs. Liebman needs flour and coffee and ten pounds of potatoes and..."

"Here, give me the list." Mr. Klein took the paper from Adam. He looked at Sammy. "Where's your friend?"

"Friend? Oh, you mean Joshua. He's not my friend, he's my cousin. He stayed at the hotel." Sammy and Adam had ducked out before Joshua knew they were leaving, but he didn't want to say that to Mr. Klein.

"Okay. Give me a minute to get this stuff together." He walked to the back of the store.

When he returned, Sammy asked, "Mr. Klein, do you know if Zeke's had any new...*problems?*"

"He was in earlier to get his mail but didn't mention anything. I'd stay out of his business if I were you. He likes to keep things private."

"That reminds me, Mr. Katzenblum asked us to check if there was mail for him," Adam said.

"Nope, 'fraid not. Here's your order, boys." Mr. Klein pushed the box towards them.

As they loaded the supplies into the wagon, a grizzled man in shabby blue overalls walked out of the building across the street.

"Adam!" Sammy whispered. "It's Amos!"

Amos crossed the street a few feet from them and disappeared around the corner.

"We've got to—"

"We can't follow him, Sammy. Mrs. Liebman would kill me if I just left the wagon with all the supplies here. And we have to get back quick so she can use this stuff for dinner."

Sammy sighed, staring at the corner. "Did you notice his hand?" Sammy asked as they settled in the wagon. "It's bandaged."

Adam flicked the reins and Simon trotted forward. "There was blood on the chicken coop post, remember? Maybe it was his."

"Well, if he is the Headless Horseman, we'll find out tonight."

CHAPTER EIGHTEEN

GOING HOME?

As Sammy left the kitchen after lunch, his father stopped him. "Sammy, your stepmother and I have decided that you should come home with us when we leave tomorrow."

"What!" Sammy looked at him in disbelief. "Why?"

"You are getting into too much trouble here."

"Did Aunt Pearl say that?"

"Your aunt thinks you are bad for Joshua. I think you are wasting your time. Jumping into the swimming pool in your clothes. Dancing with the tummler! Chasing horses without heads!"

"The horse had a head. It was the rider who didn't," Sammy mumbled.

"Enough!" His father clapped his hands. "Do what you

have to do today. Tomorrow we are going back to New York."

"I can't go back to the city." It was after lunch and Adam and Sammy were getting ready for their daily jump into the pool. "Aunt Pearl's behind this. She thinks I'm a bad influence on her precious Joshua."

"Aren't you?"

Sammy frowned. "When I first came here from Poland, Joshua called me a Greenie and treated me like I'd crawled out of the sewer. Now he wants to be one of *us*. Adam, I've got to get Papa to change his mind. But how?"

"Let me think about it," said Adam. "Are you ready? Let's go to the pool.

They ran to the deep end and jumped in. Sammy sank to the bottom, then pushed himself up and burst through the water to loud applause. He climbed up the ladder onto the deck and made a show of shaking off the water, then pretended to lose his balance and fell in again. On the opposite side of the pool, Adam did the same. Sammy pretended to be drowning, only now he did this routine with confidence. Adam swam over and grasped him around the waist and they floundered for a minute, then swam to the side and hoisted themselves out of the pool.

"I still can't figure out why they think this is funny," Sammy whispered as they stripped off their wet clothes revealing bathing costumes that made them look like they were draped in the American flag. "When Moishe gave us these costumes, I thought he was crazy," said Sammy. "I guess he knew what he was doing."

"Moishe *always* knows what he is doing," Adam said. "Remember that, Sammy. Don't ever think he doesn't."

"Is there anything we can do to change your dad's mind?" Adam asked.

"No. Papa is stubborn. Once he decides something, that's the way it is. I have to convince him that the Liebmans really need me and that I won't get into trouble."

"I'll tell him that I'll be responsible for you. After all, I'm almost fifteen; I'm practically an adult."

Sammy shrugged. "You don't know my father."

"I have a father too. He's as stubborn as a mule but I've found ways to get around him. We can at least try."

As Sammy changed into work clothes, he thought of what he could do to convince his father to let him stay.

Was it only two weeks that he'd been here? So much had happened. He hadn't wanted to come and he'd been furious when he found out that Aunt Pearl had arranged for him to work for his board. Yet it had turned out so well. Sammy liked rooming with Adam, and he'd met Moishe and the Liebmans and the Hermit.

I have to stay, Sammy thought. *I can't go back to the city and let the Awful Joshua solve the mystery without me. I have to think of some way to change Papa's mind.*

CHAPTER NINETEEN

FIRE!

"We have to do it tonight," Sammy said to Adam as they walked to their bungalow after dinner.

"Do what?" Shayna squeezed between them.

"Yeah, do what?" Joshua stepped in front of them, blocking their path. "We're The Ichabods. One for all…"

"Not so loud." Adam motioned them into the bungalow.

"We're going to the mountain men's place to investigate," Sammy said when they were safely inside with the door shut.

"Goody." Shayna clapped.

"We meet here at ten o'clock," Adam instructed. "Wear dark clothes. I'll bring the flashlight."

The night was dark. This place was beginning to spook Sammy. He could have sworn he'd heard moans coming from among the trees. He said as much to Adam who laughed and told him it was just the wind rustling the leaves. It had rained earlier and the ground was soggy under their feet. Sammy's shoes squished as he walked.

They climbed in silence. Up the hill, past the Hermit's cabin, through the trees they crept, as if there was an army on their tails.

"Halt!" Adam held up his hand. "We're here." He pointed to a clearing up ahead. "That's their place."

"What are we looking for?" Shayna whispered as they moved cautiously into the opening.

Sammy cupped a hand over his ear. "Hear that?"

"I hear a horse," she said as a loud whinny filled the air, followed by the sound of stomping hooves.

"That's what we're looking for. I want to see if the horse has a white scar on its right shoulder."

"Get back." Adam motioned for them to duck behind the trees as a figure lumbered into the clearing.

"Amos, ain't ya fed that animal yet?"

"I'm lookin' fer the sack of feed," a voice replied.

"Well, do it! I wanna get some sleep." The voice

retreated followed by the slam of a door.

"Here ya go, buddy," came the second voice. Then it too retreated into the house.

They waited until both men were inside. "All of you stay here," Sammy ordered. "Adam, give me the flashlight. I'm going to look at that horse."

"I'm coming with you," Shayna said.

"No! It's dangerous for two of us. I can sneak there and back without them seeing me." Before she could protest, Sammy darted out of the trees and across the yard to the fence where the horse was tethered. The animal's nose was buried in its feedbag. It looked up as Sammy approached. He aimed the flashlight at its shoulder, turned it on, and stared. "That's it!" he whispered. He turned the flashlight off and ran back to the trees, followed by the sound of the horse snorting and stomping its foot.

"That's the one—I saw the scar on its shoulder," he panted when he reached the others. "That's the Headless Horseman's horse."

"It all makes sense—they don't like the Hermit, they have the horse, and Amos's cut is from hurting himself on the Hermit's chicken coop post," Adam concluded.

"We did it!" Joshua cheered. "Now all we have to do is

find enough proof to bring to Sheriff Miller."

The door to the cabin opened and Amos stepped outside. "Who's out there?"

They crouched down.

Amos walked over to the horse and patted its nose. "It's just you, Ginny, feelin' yer oats?" He chuckled and went back inside.

"Come on," Adam said. "Let's get out of here."

Halfway down the mountain, Sammy stopped.

"What's that?" He pointed to a column of smoke rising up beyond the trees. He bolted forward, tripped over a tree root, regained his balance, and kept running. The others were right behind him. They crashed into the clearing and stared.

The Hermit was in front of his cabin, using a blanket to beat at flames that were licking the side of the chicken coop. His face was shiny with sweat, and when he looked at them, his eyes were red from the smoke.

"Water!" He coughed and pointed to an overturned bucket.

Sammy grabbed it and ran to the water pump. Grasping the handle, he pumped hard until the bucket was full and then brought it to the Hermit, who threw it on the fire and then handed it back to Sammy to refill. The others looked for ways they could help. Shayna found another old blanket at the side of the house and handed it to the Hermit, who used it to smother the flames.

"We caught all the chickens, sir," Adam said after the fire was out. "They're back in the coop."

"Thank the Lord for small favours. I got those chickens to replace the ones I lost last time."

"What happened?" asked Sammy.

"I was just turnin' in when I heard something outside. I opened the door and saw the chicken coop on fire and some fool runnin' to his horse and takin' off."

"What'd he look like?"

"I didn't get a good look at him. But his horse had this white line that stood out clear as day on that black coat."

"Which way did he go?" Shayna asked.

The Hermit pointed down the hill. "What are you kids doing out here in the middle of the night anyway? You just don't know how to stay out of trouble, do you? Y'all did good helpin' me tonight, but I'm takin' you back down to the hotel where you belong. I need to look after this arm."

"What's wrong with it?" Sammy asked.

The Hermit winced in pain.

Now Sammy noticed that the shirt fabric on his right arm was burnt. "You hurt your arm."

"Nothing serious. I'll look after it and be right back. Wait here!" He went into the cabin.

While they were waiting, Shayna and Sammy poked around the spot where the fire had been.

"How could the mountain men have set the fire if we saw them at home just before the fire started?" asked Shayna.

"This doesn't make any sense. Maybe it's not the mountain men, then," Sammy said. "But if not them, who?"

"Hey! Look at this!" Joshua held up a horseshoe.

"Let me see that." As he walked towards Joshua, Adam stopped and picked up a small box. "And here's a matchbox." He stuffed it into his pocket as the Hermit returned.

"Come on, now. Let's get you all back."

"Keep the horseshoe," Sammy hissed to Joshua as they moved into the woods.

"What trouble are you into this time?" Mrs. Liebman stood on the porch, clucking like a mother hen.

"I don't know what they were doing on the hill, but

they helped me save my chicken coop," the Hermit said.

"*Got in himmel*," Mrs. Liebman slapped her forehead. "What happened, Zeke?"

"Someone set it on fire." Seeing her alarm, he added, "We're all fine. It's going to be hard work repairing it, though."

"We can help you with that, sir," offered Sammy.

"And, Shayna, just *what* were you all doing out in the middle of the night? And you, Adam?"

"I'm sorry, Mrs. Liebman. We were just…"

Uncle Milton and Aunt Pearl came out onto the porch. "Joshua, where were you?" his mother demanded. "Sammy, are you getting my son in trouble?"

Things can't get worse. Sammy thought, then jumped as his father marched up to him. *They're worse!*

"Pack your things. We are leaving now!"

"No, Papa, please! I have to stay and help! Just listen—"

"I will not hear of it!"

"Ruben," Tanta Martha walked up from behind him. She spoke softly and put a hand on her husband's arm. "It looks like they've been through a lot tonight. Let's just hear what he has to say."

Sammy's father looked from his wife to his son. "So,

what is so important?"

Sammy pointed to the Hermit. Uncle Milton had brought out a first aid kit and was treating his arm. "That's Zeke. His chicken coop got damaged tonight and we promised to help him fix it. He's hurt and he needs our help. He lives all by himself on the top of the hill."

His father looked up at Zeke and then at Martha's pleading face. He closed his eyes. He sucked in his breath, rubbed his chin, and rocked back and forth on his heels, as if praying. Finally, he lifted his head and spoke. "Fine, you will stay and help." He turned to Aunt Pearl. "You will take responsibility for him?"

"If I have to," she sneered.

Mrs. Liebman shook a finger under Adam's nose. "No more monkeyshine business, you hear me?"

"Monkey business," Adam corrected. "Yes, Mrs. Liebman."

"You do your work here and then go up to Zeke's place and help him. Yes?"

Sammy lowered his head to hide his smile. "Yes 'm."

His father sighed. "So, you will stay. But no more trouble."

"Yes, Papa," Sammy said meekly. But in his head, he was silently cheering.

CHAPTER TWENTY

A HIDDEN CLUE

"That worked out okay," Adam said as he and Sammy washed up the next morning.

"Okay? The Liebmans were furious and my father threatened to ship me off right then and there!"

"But you're staying, aren't you? You're not going back to the city."

Sammy smiled. "Yeah, you're right." His expression turned to worry. "But whoever is terrorizing the Hermit means business. Setting his coop on fire was really dangerous." He looked at the sky. The sun was halfway up. "Come on. Everyone'll be down for breakfast. We'd better wash up and change our clothes fast."

"Mama really knows how to make a kid feel bad." Shayna

swept past the two boys as she placed pitchers of sour cream on the tables.

"Got a tongue-lashing last night?" Adam shot her a sympathetic look.

"You're lucky your parents don't live here." She sighed. "Let's meet at the rock out back after breakfast. We need to get down to business and solve this case." She gave them a spirited smile and sashayed back into the kitchen.

"Uh oh," Sammy said as he saw Aunt Pearl making a beeline towards him. Joshua and Leah followed.

"Joshua, Leah—go in and take your seats." She turned to Sammy as they walked past. "Young man, after last night's shenanigans, I will be watching you like a hawk. From now on, you will tell me *everything* you do and *everywhere* you go." She put her face so close that Sammy could smell the tooth powder she'd used. "*Do you understand?*"

He nodded. "Yes, Aunt Pearl."

"And I know it was your idea to take Joshua out at night—don't think I don't! He'll be watching you too and reporting to me. Now, I'd like a cup of tea with my breakfast," she said, walking towards the table at the other end of the room and sitting down.

Shayna walked over to Sammy. "I heard what she said

just now. How about I take care of her table this morning?"

Sammy gratefully accepted. He wasn't sure he'd be able to stop himself from lunging at Joshua and turning him into the next headless ghost.

Sammy was the first to arrive at the rock. It was behind the main building, shaded by a huge maple tree, and flat, so they could sit around it and discuss important things.

Shayna arrived next. "Your aunt should be outlawed."

"You'll be rid of her after the summer. I'm stuck with her for life. What did she do now?"

"Sent me back to the kitchen four times. First, the bagels were too hard. The next batch was under baked. Then Joshua didn't like his eggs—too runny—so I had to ask my mother to make him a new batch."

"That's three. What was the fourth time?"

Shayna giggled. "You won't believe it."

"Go on."

"She found a chip in her coffee cup. She wanted me to find the missing piece to make sure she hadn't swallowed it."

"And did you? Find it?" Sammy was laughing so hard he could barely get the words out.

"No."

"What's so funny?" Adam joined them on the rock.

"My Aunt Pearl was frightened by a chip in her coffee cup." Sammy wiped his eyes. "When we first came to New York, she brought us her old dishes. Every one of them had a chip in it."

"Do you think she swallowed them all? Maybe that's why she's so grumpy." Shayna grinned.

Sammy looked up to see Joshua approaching.

"Why did you tell your mom that last night was my idea?"

"I didn't!"

"That's not what she told me."

"She figured it was your idea. I just didn't correct her."

"You're such a jerk!"

"Name-calling is for babies!"

"There you are." Sammy's father marched up to them, followed by Tanta Martha. "We are leaving now. I told your Aunt Pearl to let me know the minute you get into trouble again."

"Why do you think I'll get into trouble?"

"Trouble finds you, Sammy. But remember, you don't have to always say yes."

Sammy gritted his teeth. "Bye, Papa." He stood and gave him a hug.

He whispered in Sammy's ear. "Say something nice to your stepmother."

Sammy looked at Tanta Martha. She was as ill at ease as he was. And suddenly, Sammy realized that she too was in an awkward situation. She had inherited him when she'd married Papa and, to be honest, he was no prize. He was stubborn and always getting into some sort of mischief. Maybe she was having second thoughts about this stepmother business.

"Have a good trip back to the city. And say hi to Malka. Tell her not to have the baby until I get home."

"Babies come when *they* want to." She pulled Sammy's head to her chest. "Be good," she whispered. "Don't give your father more worries."

"I won't. I promise." Before she pulled away, Sammy tugged her arm back down and whispered, "Thank you for helping me last night. I'm glad you were here. I'm...I'm glad Papa has someone again."

"Oh!" Her hand flew to her face. She looked at Sammy and this time there were tears in her eyes.

After they had left, Sammy sank beside the rock. "Whew. I thought they'd changed their minds about letting me stay here."

"All right boys, back to the case. What've we got?" Shayna got to her feet and looked down on them. "We know it's not the mountain men. They couldn't be in two places at once. So, who else could it be?" She reached into the pocket of her shorts and pulled out a pad of paper and a pencil. "I'll be the secretary. Did you guys bring the clues from last night?"

"Right here," said Adam, as he pulled the matchbox out of his pocket.

"Pass it to me." Shayna stretched out her hand.

"It's from the café in Loch Sheldrake. It's probably not the Hermit's."

Shayna read the café name on the cover of the matchbox and wrote it in her notepad. She passed the clue to Sammy.

Sammy slid the match compartment open. There were only a few matches left inside. Scrawled in ink near the edge of the inner box was a word.

"It says, 'Abby's'," read Shayna. "Abby's...as in, Abby's Acres?"

"Wait, I know that bungalow colony. Isn't that Mrs.

Schwartz's?" asked Adam.

"Right! Abigail Schwartz," confirmed Shayna.

Sammy thought back to when he'd heard that name. "Didn't you say Moishe was staying there, Adam?"

"Yeah, this summer he is."

"You don't think Moishe is the horseman, do you?" Sammy was really growing fond of Moishe. He was like a singing and performing mentor to him.

"Well, Moishe doesn't know how to ride a horse and he was with us when the horseman showed up on the Fourth of July. Besides, he wouldn't write his own address down on his matchbox," Adam reasoned.

"Still, we need to keep an eye on Moishe," said Shayna.

"Here's another clue." Joshua produced the horseshoe. "I hid it in the bushes so my parents wouldn't see it," he explained.

Mrs. Liebman popped her head out the back door of the main house. "What are you all doing? You think maybe the coop will build itself? Zeke's expecting you this afternoon. Go!"

"Hide the horseshoe," Sammy ordered Joshua. "It may be important."

CHAPTER TWENTY-ONE

THE HERMIT SPEAKS

The Ichabods climbed the hill and found the Hermit looking down into his well.

"What happened?" They ran over to him.

"They try to set my chickens on fire, and now they dump garbage into my well. They are not going to scare me off that easy." He shook his fist in the air.

"We'll catch him." Sammy stared down into the murky water.

"Listen here—I don't need y'all to catch nobody. How about you just stick to helpin' me clean up this mess?"

For the rest of the afternoon, Sammy and Adam helped the Hermit clear the debris from the well, and Shayna and Joshua cleaned out the chicken coop. After they finished, the Hermit came outside with a tray bearing a pitcher of lemonade and glasses. He set it down on a tree stump to the right of the door, sat on the ground, and motioned for them to join him.

He took a white handkerchief from his shirt pocket and wiped his forehead. "Whewee… sure is hot. Reminds me of summers in Georgia."

Sammy took a gulp of lemonade. It was sweet and tangy with bits of fruit that tickled his tongue. He watched the Hermit empty his glass in a single long swig and then wipe his mouth with the back of his hand.

Sammy set his glass down and leaned forward. "What was it like in Georgia? I mean, what…?"

"You want to know what it was like bein' a slave?"

Sammy's cheeks burned. "Yeah, I guess that's what I mean," he stammered. He never would've had the nerve to ask him any personal questions. But the more time he spent with the Hermit, the more curious he became. To his surprise, Sammy was beginning to like him.

The Hermit shook his head and sighed. "Bein' a slave means that you do what your master says, eat what he lets you eat, and wear the clothes he gives you. If you're lucky enough to be a house slave—working in the big house instead of the fields—you do the Mistress's bidding too."

"Were you a house slave?" Joshua asked.

"No. I worked in the fields. It was hard work, pickin' cotton, but I was young and big and strong." He paused, then resumed in a quiet voice. "When you're a slave, you're someone's property, period. You do what they say, if you don't want trouble."

"Like we have to listen to Mrs. Liebman?" Sammy meant it as a joke but Zeke took it seriously.

"You ain't got no idea what trouble is," he fumed.

Anger boiled up in Sammy. "Yes, I do!" he yelled. "I was in a war. Our village was invaded by soldiers. My mother died."

Zeke looked at Sammy in surprise and his gaze softened. "Yes, well then I guess you do know trouble."

Adam drained his glass and set it on the ground. "How did you escape?"

"Now that's a story." The Hermit gave a rueful smile. "I'd already tried it once. Been caught and whipped. But I was determined to be free. I was illiterate because it was illegal to teach slaves to read and write. I learned after I came here."

"If you couldn't read a map, how did you know where to go?" Shayna asked.

"I used the stars as my map." He pointed up at the sky. "The North Star is the guide. You know them stars you call the Big Dipper? We called them 'the drinking gourd'. There was a song slaves used to sing to help them find the way to freedom. For example, the lyrics say to follow the river bed until you get to two hills."

"Wow! The song gave you instructions about where to go," Sammy said in wonder.

"Yes it did. We paid attention to those words. And there were other hints. Messages whispered from one slave to another. Some who had escaped even came back to help us. Not everyone made it. They sent search parties with dogs to find us, but I got out of Georgia and came all the way to New York."

"Do you have any family?"

"I have a married daughter in Chicago. I just got a letter sayin' she's had a baby, so I guess that makes me a grandpa." He smiled proudly. "It'd be real nice to see them. Maybe one day I'll build a little cabin for them so they can come visit me."

Sammy wanted to ask him more about his life on the plantation, but Zeke abruptly got to his feet. "That's enough for today. Thank you for all your help. I can handle the rest." He turned and went into the house.

Sammy and Adam were setting the tables for dinner when they heard Mrs. Liebman shout in frustration.

"What is it? What's wrong?" Adam and Sammy rushed into the kitchen.

Mrs. Liebman was cleaning up a mess on the floor. "I went to check on the linens while the strudel cooled for dusting and I come back and find it smashed on the floor. Oy! What a mess."

Sammy helped pick up some of the broken dishes.

"My Bubbie Bluma doesn't want me to use her recipe. She did this. Last week, she poured so much salt in the chicken soup I had to throw it out. Another time she put salt in the sugar bowl. And once she even put lard," she wrinkled her nose, "that's *pig fat*, into the container where I keep *schmaltz*, the chicken fat I cook with. I had to throw it all out." She wiped her hands on her apron. "Now, what will I do for dessert?"

"Sammy and I will pick berries and you can serve those with sugar," Adam suggested.

"Okay, hurry. Shayna and I will finish setting the tables."

"Where will we get enough berries to feed the whole hotel?" Sammy asked as he and Adam headed for the road. "The wild bushes are nearly all picked out."

"Mr. Rothstein grows them. We'll ask his permission and tell him to bill Mr. Liebman for whatever we pick."

"Are you sure that's a good idea? They don't seem to get along."

"We're not asking for them for free, Sammy."

"We told Mrs. Liebman we were going to *pick* them."

"We are. We're just not picking them in the woods. Besides, Mr. Liebman will be happy to pay for the berries to keep Mrs. Liebman happy."

They had reached the Rothstein farm. As they walked up the drive to the farmhouse, Sammy noticed how prosperous the place looked. On his right, cornstalks lined up like soldiers in a parade were guarded by a fierce-looking scarecrow dressed in blue overalls, a red shirt, and battered straw hat. To his left, cows grazed in a grassy meadow studded with bluebells and yellow buttercups. Ahead of them was the farmhouse—a square white building with green shutters—and a short distance away was a red barn with white doors and a steeply slanted black roof. They mounted the steps to the farmhouse door and knocked.

The door opened and Mr. Rothstein stared down at the boys. "What do you want?"

"Mrs. Liebman needs some berries for dessert tonight and we wondered if we might pick some here. Mr. Liebman will pay you, of course."

"Tell him to keep his money."

"Please, Mr. Rothstein. We really need your help. All the guests are expecting a dessert."

Mr. Rothstein ran a hand through his hair and sighed. "Wait a minute." He disappeared into the house and returned a moment later with a large basket filled with strawberries. "Take these and get out."

Adam took the basket. "Thank you, sir. I'm sure Mrs. Liebman will be very grateful."

Mr. Rothstein grunted and shut the door.

"It's a shame that Mrs. Liebman and her brother are enemies," Sammy said as they walked back down the drive. "Adam, look." Sammy stopped and pointed over the fence to a pair of horses grazing in the pasture. "That black horse—it's got a white mark on its shoulder. Do you think...?" He walked towards to the fence. Sammy looked closer at the faded white mark. "It looks smeared, like it's made of powder or something."

Adam peered at the mark. "Why would Mr. Rothstein put powder on his horse? Unless…"

"Uh oh." Sammy said as Mr. Rothstein emerged from a side door of the house. "Let's get out of here." He pulled on Adam's arm and they hurried down the drive, Adam cradling the basket of berries and Sammy daring one quick look back at the horse.

"Mrs. Liebman, I don't think your grandmother ruined the strudel." Sammy handed her the basket of berries.

"Who else?" She dumped the strawberries into a colander and rinsed them under cold water.

"Even if it were possible, why would she do that to you, her own granddaughter?"

"My Bubbie Bluma, may she rest in peace, was a wonderful cook and baker. She was happy to share her recipes but always with one or two ingredients missing."

"Why would she do that?"

"So people would say, 'no one can cook like Bluma'. But I fooled her. I am also a good cook, so I figured out what was missing and added it. This makes her angry."

"But she's dead."

"So?" Mrs. Liebman placed a hand on Sammy's shoulder. "You don't think the departed can reach out to us?"

"I...I don't know," he stammered.

"Well I do. Bubbie Bluma wants me out of this hotel. But I won't let her scare me away." She handed him the berries. "Here. Put one big spoonful into each bowl and sprinkle on some sugar. But don't be too generous. I want to have enough to go around."

CHAPTER TWENTY-TWO

A SPECIAL GUEST

Moishe was waiting for the boys in the casino. "We," he said, jumping up and down and clapping his hands, "are having a special guest tonight."

"Who?"

"Who?" Moishe held out his hands. "Who? Who?"

"You sound like an owl," Adam said. "Tell us already."

Moishe mugged an insulted face. He was obviously enjoying his moment of suspense. He paused, then at Sammy's impatient gesture, he blurted out the name. "Eddie Cantor."

"The vaudeville star?" Sammy had seen the performer's name on the billboard at the Palace Theatre on Broadway and had heard his voice on Uncle Milton's gramophone records. "He's a big star. Why is he coming here?"

"Well, he's not exactly coming here." Moishe shuffled his feet. "He's visiting at Grossinger's Terrace Hill House up the road. But I'm going to invite him to come to hear *you*." He pointed at Sammy. "So be ready to put on a great show tonight."

"Do you know him?" Sammy was impressed.

"Well, sort of," Moishe mumbled under his breath. He pulled out a handkerchief and wiped his forehead. As he did, Sammy noticed something strange.

"What's on your sleeve?" Sammy asked. "It looks like chalk."

Moishe looked embarrassed. "It's nothing—a little powdered sugar from the kitchen. I was sampling the strudel."

But it got ruined before Mrs. Liebman could put sugar on it, Sammy thought. He looked at Adam and saw that he was thinking the same thing. "We'll talk later," Adam mouthed. Sammy nodded and turned back to Moishe.

The crowd in the parlor was bigger than usual. Word had gotten out about a surprise guest and even Mr. Katzenblum, who usually avoided the entertainments, was there. As Sammy waited for the crowd to settle down, he scanned the room for Moishe but couldn't find him. Sammy looked at Mrs. Liebman, who shrugged and then motioned for him to start on his own. So he stepped forward and bowed.

"Hello, everyone." Sammy made a sweeping gesture with his hand. "Welcome to the Pine Grove's super spectacular variety show." *What variety?* he thought. *It's only me.*

"Sing already," a man in the front row called out.

"Yes, Sammy, give us a song," said Molly. She put her horn to her ear and waggled it at him.

"Yes, Sammy, *give us a song*." Joshua echoed with a grin.

Sammy shot him a warning look. Then he turned to Shayna who was sitting at the piano. "What should I sing?"

"How about 'Toot Toot Tootsie Goodbye'?" came a voice from the back of the room. Sammy saw Moishe cut through the crowd, followed by a very thin man in a light brown suit, a round bowler hat, and a brown bow tie.

"Sammy, I want you to meet Mr. Eddie Cantor," said Moishe.

"Hello, Sammy." Mr. Cantor rolled his eyes so the pupils circled in opposite directions.

"Wow, I've never seen anyone do that," Sammy said.

Mr. Cantor shook Sammy's hand. "Are you going to

sing with me?"

By now, the audience was clapping and hollering and stamping their feet. Mr. Cantor was obviously well known and liked.

"How did you get him to come here?" Sammy whispered to Moishe.

"I told him that Mrs. Liebman makes the best strudel in the Catskills." Moishe winked. Then he pushed Sammy forward. "Get up there and sing."

Eddie Cantor was standing next to the piano. He turned to Shayna. "What's your name?"

"Shayna," she replied in a soft voice.

"Okay, Shayna, will you play a song for Eddie?" And with that, he began to sing.

Toot, toot, Tootsie, goodbye.

Toot, toot, Tootsie, don't cry.

The choo choo train that takes me

Away from you, no words can tell how sad it makes me...

He motioned for Sammy to join in.

Kiss me, Tootsie, and then

Do it over again...

Sammy watched as Eddie Cantor broke into a soft shoe dance. Tapping his feet, and waving his arms, Sammy followed him and they sang and danced until Eddie Cantor ended the song with a flourish. The audience clapped and clapped. "More!" they shouted. "More!"

"Shayna, play another song for Eddie. Can you play 'If You Knew Susie'?"

Shayna nodded.

Eddie jumped up and down, clapping his hands and rolling his eyes, as he sang the first verse.

"Sing, Sammy." Moishe poked him in the ribs.

Sammy stood next to Mr. Cantor and followed along. One, two, three—he moved his feet and then waved his arms. He did everything that Eddie Cantor did except roll his eyes.

"How do you roll your eyes like that?" Sammy asked, when they had finished.

"It's a gift, kid. You've either got it or you don't." Eddie patted Sammy on the shoulder. "But don't worry. You have enough talent without the eye roll." He turned to Moishe. "Now where's that strudel you promised me?"

Later, when he was leaving, Eddie Cantor pulled Sammy aside. "You're good, kid, real good. You've got a strong voice and a good sense of rhythm." He handed Sammy a card. "Come see me at when you get back to the city."

Sammy felt as if he were floating on air. The great Eddie Cantor said he was a talented singer. That he might one day be able to entertain people in a theatre.

"So, what did I tell you?" Moishe came up to Sammy. "You're a born entertainer, Sammy. Stick with me and I'll make you a star. Mrs. Liebman," he called, walking over to the porch where she was leaning on the rail. "You should have people like Eddie up here all the time. You'd have more guests. You could build a bigger place."

"I don't want a bigger place. How many times do I have to tell you, Moishe, that we like things the way they are? Whew, it's hot." She fanned her face with her hand. "We run a hotel, not a vaudeville show. Next you'll bring up some hotsie-totsie showgirls."

"I'd like that," Adam joined her at the rail.

"Me too." Sammy rubbed his hands together.

"*Oy vey*. That's all I need. Hotsie-totsies in skimpy costumes kicking up their legs in my casino."

Moishe laughed. "You are missing a golden opportunity. Right this minute, Eddie Cantor is down the road with the Grossingers."

"So, let him. Malke Grossinger is a cook, like me," Mrs. Liebman snorted. "Trust me, she won't want the hotsie-totsies either."

"The Grossingers' daughter Jenny likes the entertainment," said Moishe.

"So let *her* do it!" She paused. "What's that?" Mrs. Liebman jumped as the thunder of hooves filled the air.

Sammy whirled around in time to see a black stallion with a white scar on its shoulder galloping towards them. As it approached, the rider pulled back on the reins. A hollow voice rumbled out, "Beware!", followed by an eerie, high-pitched laugh. People ran out of the house to see what the commotion was all about. With the sharp crack of his whip and another burst of laughter, the rider galloped away.

"Sammy! Again with the jokes?" Mrs. Liebman glared at him.

"It wasn't me, I…"

Adam rescued him. "Have you read *The Legend of Sleepy Hollow?*"

"The what?"

"It's a story. A Headless Horseman who is the ghost of a dead soldier scares a schoolteacher named Ichabod Crane. Someone," he said, "is trying to do the same thing to the Hermit."

"And to us, it seems," said Moishe, who was still staring

in the direction taken by the horse and rider.

"Headless, shmedless...a bad joke." Mrs. Liebman turned to Moishe. "You wouldn't maybe have something to do with this?"

"Me?" Moishe rolled his eyes heavenward. "Could it be, Mrs. Liebman that your grandmother has friends...up there?"

Mrs. Liebman stared at him. "Moishe, do you think...? No! That is impossible. I'm going to bed. I've had enough excitement for one day."

After she left, Sammy turned to Moishe. "Moishe, do you know who the horseman is?"

"Me?" Moishe put his hand over his heart. "How should I know? It's been a long night. Good night, boys."

They watched him go.

"C'mon, Sammy." Adam touched his friend's arm. "Let's get to sleep. We can think about this again in the morning."

But Sammy couldn't sleep. Lying in bed, he went over and over the events of the day: Moishe's surprise guest, his performance with Eddie Cantor and being given his card, and lastly, the appearance of the Horseman. Something didn't fit. If the Horseman was terrorizing the Hermit, why had he come to the Pine Grove twice? Was he also trying to scare the Liebmans? And what was Moishe's involvement in all this? Sammy didn't know the answers, but he was determined to find out.

CHAPTER TWENTY-THREE

THE ICHABODS MEET

The morning after the Horseman's latest visit, a second family packed up their things and moved to a bungalow colony near Liberty. "We don't need so much excitement," the woman said to Mrs. Liebman when asked why they were leaving.

"I don't need it either," Mrs. Liebman called out after their retreating backs. She turned to her husband. "Maybe it is Bubbie Bluma. She is sending an evil messenger from the beyond."

"What makes you think such a thing?" Mr. Liebman took her hand.

Mrs. Liebman looked up at him. "No. It's true. She is angry. This was her place and she wants it back."

"Do you think she can run a hotel from the grave? That

is nonsense. You are smarter than that."

But Mrs. Liebman would not be convinced. "It is her, I tell you. She is angry because I am a better cook— that's what it is. She is jealous."

"Rose, darling, you are taking this too seriously," he soothed her. "Come. We'll go into the kitchen and have some tea."

Sammy watched them go. "Shayna, do you believe there's a ghost here?"

"I believe my mother thinks there's one." She twirled a strand of hair around her finger. "I never knew Bubbie Bluma, but I've heard stories that she was very stern and very proud. Especially of her cooking. Every time one of Mama's dishes gets ruined, she says it's her bubbie cursing her."

"But these are real actions—ruined strudel, lard in the schmaltz container. A ghost can't do that."

"A ghost can't do what?" Adam sauntered up to them.

"The stuff that's been happening to poor Mrs. Liebman," Sammy said. "I'm worried about her."

"SHAYNA! ADAM! SAMMY!" Mrs. Liebman came out on the porch. "You think the tables will set themselves?"

"You're worried about *her*?" joked Adam. "She sounds just fine to me."

It was time for another gathering of The Ichabods. They met at the rock after lunch. Shayna spread a red-and-white checked cloth on top of its surface and set out a tray with a pitcher of lemonade, four glasses, and a plate of sugar cookies. After everyone helped themselves, she called the meeting to order.

"How come you're the president?" Joshua demanded.

"Because I'm the oldest." Shayna said proudly.

"Adam's the oldest," he protested. "Aren't you?"

"Shayna beats me by three days. She can be the president."

"So, now that that's settled," Shayna brushed cookie crumbs off her mouth. "Do we have any new leads? We suspect that Moishe is involved somehow, but that's all we have."

"Actually," Sammy said, "let's go backwards. When we went to Rothstein's farm yesterday, we found a horse. It looked like it had a faded white streak on its shoulder, but when I looked closer, it almost looked like the streak had been drawn on with some kind of powder."

"Wait," Adam said, sitting up higher. "Moishe had white powder on his sleeve yesterday. He said it was from sampling the strudel, but we know that the strudel was ruined before he could've done that."

"So is this powder on Moishe's sleeve the same powder that is on Rothstein's horse?" Joshua asked.

Sammy frowned. "If Moishe is mixed up in this, why would he want to scare the Hermit?"

"Suspicious," said Shayna as she wrote notes in her notepad.

The group sat in silence, thinking.

Adam finally spoke. "It's not just the Hermit being terrorized now, though. The Pine Grove seems to be a target, too. Moishe said something the other night about bringing more entertainers up for the guests."

Shayna continued his line of thought. "He's just a tummler. He acts crazy and does tricks. But what if he wants to do more, like put on a vaudeville show? He would need a bigger place to do it."

"But what does that have to do with the Hermit?" asked Joshua. "Maybe he's trying to make everyone think he's being terrorized so he can get their sympathy. Have we ever seen the Hermit and the Headless Horseman at the same time?"

"Yes we have," Sammy countered. "That night the chickens got out, remember?"

"Oh, right. Maybe he hired someone to be the Headless Horseman?" Joshua offered.

"Well, it wouldn't be the mountain men, since we saw them at home with their horse just before the horseman showed up at the Hermit's place." Sammy fiddled with a piece of grass. "Besides, I don't think the Hermit wants sympathy or attention. He likes to keep things private."

"So," said Shayna. "We've got my uncle with a horse that looks like the Headless Horseman's horse, Moishe lying about a mysterious powder on his sleeve, a matchbox with Moishe's address on it, and a horseshoe."

"We should go back to the farm and get a better look at that horse." Adam jumped to his feet. "But for now, it's time to go to the pool. Let's think about all this and meet again tonight. In the meantime, let's try to figure out what Moishe is up to and keep our ears open for anybody who might be talking about anything related to the Hermit or the Horseman."

CHAPTER TWENTY-FOUR

A SERIOUS PLOT

During the first week of August, many of the guests went back to the city and new ones arrived. A few people, like Aunt Pearl, were up for the whole summer. Others came for shorter stays—a week or two—and everyone wanted the same things: lots of food and funny entertainment. So when Sammy wasn't working in the dining room, he was busy with Moishe, planning the shows.

Moishe was waiting by the piano after breakfast. "So, Sammy, what will you sing for us today? Any new ideas?"

"Not yet." Once again, Sammy wondered about Moishe. Was he really just a tummler, or was he something more?

"Sammy, there you are." Mrs. Liebman bustled into the

parlor. "Adam is going into town for supplies. Go with him to help."

"I'm sorry, Moishe." Sammy gave him a regretful look.

"No, go, go." Moishe made a shooing motion with his hands.

The general store was empty except for Mr. Klein who was standing behind the counter.

"Good afternoon, boychiks. What can I do for you today?"

"The usual. Mrs. Liebman needs some supplies." Adam handed Mr. Klein a paper.

"Hmm." Mr. Klein adjusted his glasses and ran his finger down the grocery list. "This will take me a few minutes to put together." He disappeared into the back of the store.

Sammy inhaled the scent of sawdust, fresh ground coffee, and pickles soaking in brine. The pickles reminded him of Mr. Klopchuck's Pickle Palace and Sammy's adventures with his friends on Orchard Street. His initiation into the gang was to steal a pickle from Mr. Klopchuck's wooden pickle barrel. After that, they let him play stickball with them. He missed his gang but gloated that he was having an exciting summer. *Boy, will I have stories to tell them.*

The doorbell jangled and Sheriff Miller entered. "Hello, boys. I hear you've been having some great entertainment at your place. I'll have to get out there one of these nights."

"We'd love to have you, sir." Adam turned to Sammy. "Sammy is our star."

"Really?" The sheriff looked impressed. "All the more reason for me to drop by."

Mr. Klein came back and set a box of groceries on the counter. "Morning, Sheriff. What can I do for you today?"

"Just checking to see if you've had any more trouble from those mountain men."

"You mean Amos?" Mr. Klein grimaced. "Haven't seen him in a while. Guess he and his brother are holed up in that shack of theirs."

"Well, let me know if they give you any problems." He turned to the boys. "How are things at the Pine Grove, boys?"

"Uh, oh, fine." *Should I tell him about the horseman?* Sammy thought. As if reading his mind, Adam shook his head.

"Here's your mail, Sheriff," Mr. Klein said. "That

reminds me, boys. I have a letter here for Mr. Katzenblum. It's probably the one he's been waiting for."

Adam took it and stuffed it in his pocket. "I'll give it to him. Thanks, Mr. Klein."

Adam put the groceries in the cart and then climbed on board with Sammy.

CHAPTER TWENTY-FIVE

THE FARM

"Oh good, you are back," Mrs. Liebman called out as Adam jumped down from the wagon and tied the reins to the post.

Mr. Katzenblum was sitting on the porch reading a newspaper. He looked up as the boys unloaded the wagon. "Do you have a letter for me?"

Adam pulled the envelope from his pocket and handed it to him.

"About time!" Mr. Katzenblum snatched it from Adam's hand. He turned sharply on his heel, picked up his cane, and went into the hotel.

Sammy turned to Adam. "Wow, he sure was anxious to get that letter."

"Nearly swiped my hand with it," Adam muttered as

he hauled the supplies to the kitchen. "Forget him. What we need to focus on is getting back to Rothstein's farm. Only, how are we going to get around your aunt? She's still watching you like a hawk."

"By going to bed early." Sammy grinned.

Adam gave him a puzzled look.

"When she comes to check on us, I'll be in bed fast asleep. Or at least, that's what she'll think. Then she'll go to bed. Once she's asleep, you could burn the hotel down and she wouldn't notice. So we're free."

Adam gave him a thumbs up. "Shayna and I will meet you outside the bungalow after her nightly check."

Sammy met Adam and Shayna and, to his surprise, found Joshua there too.

"He guessed what we're doing." Adam gave Sammy a sheepish look.

"What about your mother? You're going to give us all away."

"She's sound asleep. Besides," Joshua said, lowering his head, "I have to be here. I'm an Ichabod."

"One for all and all for one," Shayna said. "Let's get going."

"I brought this." Joshua held up the horseshoe he'd found at the Hermit's place. "We can see if it matches the one on Mr. Rothstein's horse."

Adam gave him an appreciative look. "Good thinking, Joshua."

Joshua beamed.

Silently, they crossed the road, walked up the path and onto the farm. Adam focused his flashlight on the ground in front of them. Sammy heard rustling noises. *Mice. Maybe snakes.* He shuddered. Then he looked ahead. The dark shape of a house was barely visible. Behind it, to the right was the barn. Sammy touched Adam's arm and pointed. Adam nodded and they turned in that direction.

"Joshua, keep watch as we check out the inside," ordered Adam.

"Why do I have to keep watch?" complained Joshua.

"Because you have the best eyesight," said Shayna sweetly.

"Oh, right." Joshua straightened his shoulders, assuming a watchman's posture. "Here's the horseshoe, Adam."

Adam took it with a nod and followed Sammy and

Shayna through the barn door ahead of them.

The inside smelled of dust, hay, and sour milk. As Sammy's eyes adjusted to the gloom, he made out two rows of stalls. Low moos told them the occupants were cows. But the stalls at the back seemed larger than the rest. Sammy walked towards them and was greeted with a loud whinny and the stomping of hooves. "Whoa," he breathed as he slid the stall door open. "Guys, look. The white streak." Sammy carefully leaned over the first stall and touched the mark on the horse's shoulder as Adam fed it sugar cubes to keep it quiet. "The streak isn't real. It's drawn on."

Adam bent down, lifted the horse's right front hoof and then the left, comparing its shoes to the one Joshua had found. "The right looks new, but look at the left one. It matches the one from the Hermit's," he announced.

"And look at this." Shayna picked up a large piece of chalk from a shelf. "And this." She plucked a black cape from a hook. "Either my uncle is the horseman or he's gotten someone to do it for him."

Sammy looked around the barn. "We'd better go before someone sees us. Everything clear, Joshua?"

"All clear," Joshua called from the door. "But I stepped in mud."

"You better hope it's mud." Adam laughed.

"Quiet!" hushed Shayna. "Let's get out of here. Should we take the chalk and cape with us?"

"No, your uncle will know something's going on. We need to catch him in the act." Sammy dusted the white powder off his hand. "What are you doing, Joshua?" Sammy asked.

"Trying to get the mud off my shoes so I don't leave muddy shoeprints for your uncle to find."

"Like these?" Shayna took the flashlight and pointed it to the ground.

Sammy looked closer. "Look at the claw mark beside every other print."

"What would make a mark like that?" Joshua wondered out loud as he smeared the last of the mud off his shoe.

"A cane." Shayna clapped her hands. "Mr. Katzenblum's cane!"

"What do we do now?" Sammy asked as they walked back to the hotel.

"Get some sleep," Adam said in a matter-of-fact voice. "We have a lot to think about. The plot of this mystery is getting thicker."

Thick like molasses, Sammy thought as Adam and he tramped towards their bungalow. *Molasses catches flies. That's what I feel like—a fly trapped in goo.*

CHAPTER TWENTY-SIX

SABOTAGE

Sammy couldn't believe how fast the summer was going. It was hard to remember that he hadn't wanted to come to the Catskills, that he'd wanted to stay in New York with his gang. But he had found a new gang here: The Ichabods. And now that it was the middle of August, he didn't want the summer to end. Adam and Sammy had stayed up late talking about the mystery of the Headless Horseman. The next morning, they headed to the main building for their chores.

"Let's organize a race for the kids in the pool later."

"Adam..." Sammy stopped walking. "What's that noise?"

"We can have a relay and then dive for coins. They'll love that."

"Adam, listen!"

Adam stopped and lifted his head. "It sounds like... frogs?"

The boys ran to the pool where they were greeted by a chorus of croaking green bodies, bouncing over the surface of the water.

Sammy slapped his forehead. "There must be hundreds of them. How did they get in here?"

"Now what has she done?"

Sammy turned as Mrs. Liebman ran up behind them. "*She* did this. She brought us a plague, like in the Bible."

"We heard the noise from the kitchen," said Shayna.

"Aaagh!" Mrs. Liebman screamed as a frog jumped from the water and landed on her foot. "Get it off me!"

Adam bent down, picked up the frog, and tossed it back in the pool. But other frogs were leaping from the pool and hopping around the deck. The noise from their croaking was deafening.

The frogs were everywhere. "What do we do?" Sammy asked Adam as Moishe and Mr. Liebman ran onto the deck.

"Arnie, look what she's done!" Mrs. Liebman gave her husband a murderous look.

"Please, Rose, stay calm."

"How can I be calm? First a horseman without a head, then my food is ruined, and now this! It's my Bubbie Bluma. *Pooh, pooh, pooh.* Such an evil spirit." She turned to Moishe. "I didn't like her when she was alive but now," she sniffed, "I...*I hate her.*"

A crowd had gathered outside the pool fence. Everyone was talking at once. Sammy heard Aunt Pearl's voice rise above the rest. "What kind of hotel is this? What is going on?"

Others joined in the chorus. "I should have stayed at Grossinger's," said Mrs. Drabinsky, a tall, thin woman who had arrived the previous week. "I paid ahead." She glared at Mr. Liebman. "I want my money back!"

Moishe pleaded with the guests to calm down. "Come, everyone." He waved. "We will have games on the lawn." Then he turned to Sammy. "After you clear up the frogs, meet me in the casino," he whispered. "We will need very good entertainment for tonight."

"Moishe, how do we get rid of these things?" Adam pleaded as the tummler began to move away.

Moishe shrugged. "How should I know? Be like Moses. Ask Pharaoh to let your people go."

"Very funny." Adam turned to Sammy. "There are fishing nets in the rowboat. I'll get them. Shayna, bring some buckets from the hotel."

"What should I do?" Joshua had just joined them.

"Help Shayna carry the buckets." Adam looked at the frogs and sighed. "Too bad they aren't kosher. We could've had frog legs for dinner."

"Has everyone settled down?" Moishe asked Sammy two hours later.

"We caught most of the frogs and put them in the lake. Others hopped away on their own."

"What about the guests?"

"The Drabinskys are leaving. Everyone else seems okay. Is Eddie Cantor coming back?"

"No," Moishe said in a sour voice. "The Pine Grove isn't important enough for him and something happened to the strudel I promised him." He looked out the window.

Sammy thought of the card tucked away in his drawer at the bungalow. "He liked my singing. He said I should look him up when I get back to New York."

"Good luck, boychik. But now, let's go over the songs for tonight. Unless we want *everyone* going to Grossinger's, we need to keep them happy."

Since the pool was closed for the day, most of the guests lounged around the casino. Adam and Sammy were walking across the lawn when they were hailed by Molly, who was sitting on the porch with a few other guests.

"Is it true? Did the Drabinskys leave this morning?" she asked, horn ready at her ear.

"Oh, uh…yes, they did." Adam scratched the back of his neck.

"First a horseman, now frogs. This place is becoming downright biblical," said Mr. Katzenblum from the other end of the porch. "This hotel is a joke. I wouldn't be surprised if it shut down before the end of the season." He picked up his cane and walked down the steps to the dirt path.

Adam and Sammy watched as he strutted down the pathway towards the main house. Adam sighed. "Okay, Sammy, we have to get back to work."

"We've got a great evening of songs tonight, so make sure to come!" Sammy called out as they left the porch.

As soon as they were far enough away, Adam huffed. "Man, that guy is such a snake."

"You said it." Sammy frowned. "We have to figure out how he's involved with the Horseman. And prove it."

CHAPTER TWENTY-SEVEN

THE LETTER

"So what was Mr. Katzenblum doing at the farm?" Shayna pondered aloud. The Ichabods were sitting around their rock after breakfast the next day.

"It has something to do with the Horseman," said Sammy.

"Do you think he knows the Hermit?" asked Joshua.

"I can't think of how they'd be connected, but we know he's not a fan of the hotel. He's made that pretty clear," said Adam.

Sammy scratched his head. "There's got to be something important in that letter. We have to get a hold of it."

"How?" Shayna asked. "Where do you think Mr. Katzenblum keeps it?"

"It must be in his room," said Adam.

Joshua looked up at the house. "How are we going to get inside his room?"

"Shayna, isn't there a spare key?" asked Sammy.

"Mama has a master key to all the rooms but she wears it on a loop around her waist. But there's another way to get there. Follow me." They walked around the building. "That's his window," Shayna pointed. "Look what's in front of it."

"A tree. So what?" Sammy said.

"You've never climbed a tree?" Shayna laughed. She turned to Joshua. "*You* are going to climb up this tree and get into his room."

"*Me?*"

"You're the only one small enough to fit through the window," Adam said.

"No way! What if he's inside?"

"I'll distract him," Shayna said. "I'll get him out of the main house. Then I'll give you a signal and," she swooped her hands skyward, "up you go."

"How do you know the window's open?"

"He's always complaining about the heat. He keeps it open."

"But I've never climbed a tree," Joshua wailed. "And I

don't like heights."

"Don't worry, Joshua," Adam said. "Sammy will climb it with you and I will stand underneath to catch you if you fall."

"That's supposed to make me feel better?"

Sammy put on a fake smile. "I'm sure your big head will break your fall."

"Hey! You can't make me do this, you know."

"Joshua," Sammy said, gritting his teeth. "We need your help. Please just do this for us?"

His cousin remained silent for a second, before nodding. "Okay. For The Ichabods."

After dinner, everyone moved onto the porch. The sweltering heat hadn't subsided for the evening, so Shayna convinced Moishe to move his tummler act down by the lake. As everyone made their way down to the cooler area, Sammy, Adam, and Joshua quietly snuck off to the tree.

Adam hoisted Joshua up to the first branch.

"Okay, Joshua. Start climbing."

"Aren't you coming with me, Sammy?" Joshua asked nervously.

"I'll be right behind you. We've got to hurry, though.

Moishe is expecting me to sing once he's done his jokes."

"All right," Adam said. "I'll stand guard. Wait." He handed Sammy the flashlight. "You'll need this when you're inside."

Sammy slipped it into the waistband of his shorts, grabbed onto a branch, and hoisted himself up. "Okay, Joshua. Let's go."

Joshua made his way up the tree slowly. He looked down at Sammy and then immediately hugged the trunk and shut his eyes. "Ah! I don't think I can do this."

"Calm down. Take a breath and keep your eyes on the tree."

"Okay," Joshua replied shakily. He opened his eyes, focused his gaze upward, and continued climbing. He finally reached the branch that would lead them into Mr. Katzenblum's room. "Now what?"

Sammy climbed onto the branch next to Joshua's. "Can you walk on it like a tightrope?"

Joshua shook his head.

"All right. Then how about you sit on it with your legs on either side and inch along?"

"Okay." He took a deep breath. "I think I can do that."

"Good, just don't look down."

Joshua straddled the branch. He slowly edged closer to the window and finally made it across. The window to Mr. Katzenblum's room was narrow but just wide enough for Joshua to squeeze through.

After Joshua was safely inside, Sammy shifted over and straddled the end of the branch by the window. "Here, take the flashlight so you don't trip. And be fast. I don't know how long Shayna can keep Mr. Katzenblum distracted."

Joshua turned on the flashlight and looked around the room. There was a single bed, neatly made up with a white bedspread, an oak dresser, a desk, and a cane-backed chair. He went to the desk and shined the light along its surface. But the only thing there was a newspaper.

"Check the drawers," Sammy hissed.

Joshua opened the top drawer and pulled out a white envelope. "Found it!" He closed the drawer. Suddenly the door opened.

Joshua dropped to the floor and squeezed under the desk.

Sammy ducked down so his head was below the window.

Mr. Katzenblum flipped a switch, flooding the room with light. "Now where did I put that cane?" he muttered.

"Mr. Katzenblum!" Shayna knocked at his door.

"What is it?" he growled.

"You left your cane in the dining room," Shayna said sweetly.

"Give it to me."

"I'm sorry. I left it downstairs."

"As usual, rotten service," Mr. Katzenblum grumbled. He stepped into the hall and shut the door.

Joshua waited a minute to make sure the man wasn't coming back. Then he ran to the window. "I've got it. Let's go."

Sammy clutched the branch with both hands. He inched backwards to the trunk, then carefully turned, wrapped his arms around it, and made his way down the tree. Joshua backed out the window and followed Sammy's path to the ground. They met Adam at the bottom.

Shayna was waiting for them at the bungalow after the show. "I tried to keep him at the lake but he insisted on coming back for his cane. Good thing I hid it before he noticed he didn't have it. Did you get the letter?"

Joshua pulled the letter out of his pocket and waved it in the air.

"Yes! Open it up," Shayna leaned forward. Everyone held their breath as Joshua unfolded the single sheet of paper.

"Wow! Oh boy, this is really good." Joshua whistled.

"WHAT DOES IT SAY?" the others shouted.

"Here, let me read it." Sammy grabbed the letter. "It's from someone at the Port Authority of New York and New Jersey. It says that the Port Authority is building a tunnel under the Hudson River so that people can drive from one side to the other."

Sammy skimmed through the paragraphs. "The last bit says, 'If you're still considering buying the properties in the area we discussed, I would advise you do so as soon as possible. Prices will rise once the tunnel is announced to the public.'" He looked up and grinned. "That's our motive!"

"So Mr. Katzenblum plans on buying the hotel?" asked Joshua.

"It's more than that." Adam took the letter and looked at the end. "The letter said 'properties'. Maybe he plans to buy the farm and the Hermit's hill, too."

"Mama would never sell the hotel."

"Maybe Mr. Rothstein wants to sell his farm," said Sammy. "And Mr. Katzenblum offered him something if he could scare Mrs. Liebman and the Hermit off their properties."

"That would explain all the weird 'ghost' stuff at the hotel." Joshua said. "And Moishe would have his bigger hotel to perform shows in."

"He can become an *impresario*," Sammy said, using a word he'd learned from his Aunt Tsippi. "An impresario is a person who puts on big shows with stars like Eddie Cantor."

"So what do we do now?" asked Shayna.

Sammy looked around at his gang. "We catch this ghost."

CHAPTER TWENTY-EIGHT

THE GHOST STRIKES AGAIN

When Sammy came into the kitchen the next morning, Mrs. Liebman was standing in the middle of the room wringing her hands.

"She did this," she cried. "She doesn't want me in her kitchen."

"Who?"

"Bubbie Bluma." She waved a hand at the floor. It was littered with broken dishes.

"Mrs. Liebman, I don't think..."

"Of course you don't. You're young. You don't understand these things." She threw her hands in the air. "Arnie," she said as her husband entered the kitchen. "Maybe I *should* sell to my brother. He can deal with the ghosts."

"No, Mrs. Liebman." Sammy protested. "It isn't a ghost."

She turned to him. "You know this how?"

"I…I just feel it. Someone is doing all these things to scare you away. Don't let them do it."

"The boy is right." Mr. Liebman gave Sammy a grateful look. "For now, let's clean up. We have hungry guests and you are still the best cook in the Catskills."

"What do we serve the food in?" Mrs. Liebman pointed to a pile of broken crockery.

"The ghost only broke the milk dishes," Sammy said. "You can serve eggs in the meat dishes. Just no sour cream," he added.

"Yes. Eggs, bread, and jam. No butter." Mr. Liebman took his wife's hand. "We will go to Monticello this afternoon and buy dishes for tomorrow."

Mrs. Liebman sniffed. "I suppose so. But…such a waste of money."

"We'd better hurry." Sammy grabbed a broom and began sweeping up the shards. "You don't want Aunt Pearl complaining to everyone about bad service." He forced a laugh. "Even dealing with a fake ghost is easier than that."

"We need to get Moishe and Mr. Rothstein to stage another Headless Horseman stunt," Sammy told Adam as they cleaned up after breakfast. "That way we can unmask them and prove to everyone the Headless Horseman and Mrs. Liebman's ghost are fake. We need a meeting. Tell the others to be at the rock at ten o'clock."

"Yes, Mr. Holmes," Adam saluted. "You have solved the riddle, I presume?"

"No," Sammy laughed. "But I think I know how to do it."

Sammy was the first to reach the rock. As he scrambled onto its rough, grainy surface, he felt like an explorer searching a foreign peak. What secrets were hidden in the air of the Pine Grove and the surrounding hills?

The others arrived soon after. "Hey, feet off the table," joked Shayna.

Sammy turned around and smiled. "Yes, ma'am." He stepped off the rock and sat down with the others.

"So what's the plan?" Adam asked as he rubbed his hands together.

"Mr. Katzenblum wants to buy the hotel, but Moishe and Rothstein know Mrs. Liebman won't budge. They've been trying to scare her with ghosts because they know she's superstitious."

"Right. But the Hermit isn't superstitious. Why would they use the same trick on him?" Shayna pointed out.

"Ghost or not, the Horseman is scary, especially when you live all alone and it's nighttime," chimed Joshua. "And the costume acts like a disguise."

"So how do we catch the Horseman?" Adam asked impatiently.

"They've been trying to scare the guests away, right? So we'll stage a big show in front of lots of people. Mrs. Liebman will pretend that losing any more customers will force her to sell, and that she's afraid that the Horseman will show up at this big show."

"Oh, I get it," said Shayna. "If Moishe hears that, he'll tell Mr. Rothstein and Mr. Katzenblum. Then the Horseman will show up for sure."

Sammy grinned. "And we'll unmask him in front of everyone."

CHAPTER TWENTY-NINE

THE PLOT THICKENS

Sammy waited until late afternoon to approach Moishe. He found him on the porch talking to Mr. Katzenblum. "Moishe, may I speak to you?"

"Sure, Sammy." Moishe waved goodbye to Mr. Katzenblum and joined Sammy on the lawn. "What can I do for you, boychik?"

Sammy took a deep breath. "I want to put on another show, like the one we did the night Eddie Cantor was here."

Moishe gave him a surprised look. "I thought you didn't like performing for a big group."

"I've changed my mind. Do you think we can get another special guest?"

"Maybe." Moishe shook his head. "I'll see what I can do. When do you want to hold this extravaganza?"

"How about Saturday night? Today's Tuesday. That will give us time to rehearse."

Moishe smiled. "That's what I like about you, boycheck. You've got initiative. We'll start tonight, after dinner."

"Now what?" Adam asked when Sammy told him the news.

"We let everyone know we're having a big show here on Saturday. Make sure Mr. Rothstein hears about it too."

"Won't Moishe tell him?"

"Probably, but we don't want to take any chances."

"Okay. I'll tell him about it when I drop off the money Mr. Liebman gave me for the strawberries."

The next step, Sammy decided, was to go see the Hermit. Joshua was stuck babysitting Leah, so Sammy suggested that he and Adam go alone. They climbed the hill after lunch. "Won't they miss us at the pool?" Sammy asked.

"Shayna's covering for me. She's a great swimmer."

The day was sticky hot, and by the time they reached the Hermit's house, they were panting. "Whew, this hill gets steeper every time we climb it," Sammy gasped. They stepped from the cover of the trees and stopped short. The Hermit was hunched over, picking vegetables from his garden. He turned as they approached.

"What are you two troublemakers doing up here?"

"We need to talk to you. It's important," Sammy added.

"Well then, guess we'd better go inside." He led them into the cabin. The Hermit motioned to the table. Sammy sank onto a chair and Adam remained standing.

"Okay, so what is the problem this time?"

"We've come to help you," Sammy blurted out.

"Help me?"

"With the Headless Horseman," replied Adam. "We think we know who he is. And we think he's part of a plot to get you and the Liebmans to sell your land."

Slowly, the Hermit sank into a seat across from Sammy. He motioned for Adam to do the same. "Okay, boys, now you have my attention. Suppose you start from the beginning."

"So you see," Sammy concluded after he finished the story, "we think Mr. Rothstein is helping Mr. Katzenblum to get the Liebmans to sell the Pine Grove."

"And," added Adam, "it wouldn't hurt if Mr. Katzenblum had your property too. "That's why they're trying to scare you away. Sammy and I and the other Ichabods..."

"The Ichabods? Who in thunder are The Ichabods?"

"They're our, er, gang," Sammy said. "It's me and Adam and Shayna and Joshua. We are dedicated to protecting you and saving the Pine Grove."

"Lord, save me from well-meaning children," the Hermit muttered. Then he smiled. "You're serious, aren't you?"

"Yes, sir," the boys chorused.

"Well, in that case, what do you need me to do?"

"Just come to the big show and be ready to talk to Sheriff Miller."

After dinner that night Adam, Sammy, and Shayna stayed behind in the kitchen while Mrs. Liebman made the dough for the next day's bread.

"There's something we need to tell you."

"You and Mr. Liebman." Adam folded the cloth he had used to clean the counters and draped it over a towel rack.

"This sounds serious. Are you boys in trouble? Again?" Mrs. Liebman punched the mound of dough on the board, flipped it into a large bowl, and covered it with a damp cloth. Wiping floury hands on her apron, she turned to face them. "Should I be worried?"

"No," Adam answered. "But we need to talk to Mr. Liebman too."

Mrs. Liebman gave them a quizzical look and then walked to the kitchen door and called her husband. "Arnie, come here."

"What is it, Rose? I'm busy with the books."

"Then get unbusy. So," she turned to the boys. "What is this earth-shaking news?"

Sammy explained everything he knew about the Headless Horseman scheme and his idea to catch the culprit. "We need your help to pull this off."

"I still don't understand. You think my brother is behind all this *meshegoss* that's going on?"

Sammy took a deep breath. "It's not your grandmother. It can't be."

"You don't believe in ghosts?" Mrs. Liebman gave a bemused smile.

"No. And I suspect you don't either." Sammy looked into her eyes. "Do you?"

Mrs. Liebman looked around the kitchen at the pots and pans hanging from hooks and the ceramic bowls she used to make bread, and she smiled. "I believe in ghosts. They are part of us—part of everything we do."

Sammy thought of his mother. Was her ghost watching over him? He hoped so. "So, maybe your grandmother's ghost can help us?"

"She always liked my brother Nathan the best. A boy," she said, "carries on the family name."

"Thanks, Mama." Shayna muttered.

"Shayna, darling, I am not like my grandmother." Mrs. Liebman pulled Shayna into a hug.

"Enough with the ghosts." Mr. Liebman looked at Sammy, arms folded across his chest. "I know about you, young man. You have a wild imagination. Your aunt has told me about the trouble you caused your father. That's why she brought you up here—to give him some peace this summer. And now you are causing us trouble?"

"Please, Mr. Liebman," Adam pleaded. "I know this all sounds crazy, but it's true. If it isn't, I promise we'll never bother you again."

"Arnie," Mrs. Liebman looked up at her husband. "Maybe the children have the right idea."

"We saw the horse and the costume at the farm," Shayna said.

"And we have the letter about the tunnel," Sammy added.

Mrs. Liebman sank into a chair. She turned to face her husband. "Let's try what the boys suggest. If it is true, better we should know. If not, we'll have a laugh and these two," she pointed at Sammy and Adam, "can peel potatoes for the rest of the summer."

CHAPTER THIRTY

SETTING THE TRAP

"What do you mean you're having second thoughts about the show?" Moishe barked. He and Sammy were in the lounge, by the piano. In an hour, Sammy would go to the pool, which had been frog-free since the incident. But now was the time he'd set aside to speak to Moishe.

"Mrs. Liebman's worried that the Headless Horseman will come like he did the last time we had a big show. She says that if she loses any more customers, she's going to give up and sell this place." Sammy tried to look really worried.

Moishe gave him a long, hard stare. "Leave Mrs. Liebman to me. I will handle her." Moishe looked like he was trying hard to hide a smile. "Sammy, don't listen to her. She's a worrier. We'll put on a show and everything will be fine." He patted Sammy's head. "Trust me."

"Shayna, your mother did a good job. Moishe believes her," Sammy told The Ichabods when they met at the rock later that afternoon.

"I saw him and Mr. Katzenblum whispering on the porch after he left you," Shayna reported.

"So, we've planted the seeds," said Adam. "Now we have to wait and see what grows."

That night The Ichabods met in the boys' room. Adam had gotten paper, pen, and ink from Mr. Liebman and they set about making flyers to advertise the show. "We'll pass these out to all the hotels in the area." Adam held up the finished page:

Come to the Best Show in the Catskills

Singing, Dancing, and

a Surprise Guest.

Saturday at 8 p.m.

at the Pine Grove Kosher Hotel

"Now all we need is a show," Sammy sighed. "And a surprise guest."

"Moishe did say he'd get someone as good as Eddie

Cantor, didn't he?" asked Joshua.

"No one is as good as Eddie Cantor."

"Let's leave that up to Moishe," Shayna suggested. "Sammy, are you ready to sing?"

"More than ever."

CHAPTER THIRTY-ONE

THE MAIN EVENT

The casino was full when Sammy arrived. The flyers had worked. People had come from other hotels and farms in the area. Even Sheriff Miller and the Hermit were there. When Moishe asked him why, Sammy told him he'd personally invited them. He didn't, however, tell him why.

Moishe had assembled an entire band. There was a trumpet player, a drummer, a man playing a piccolo, and another on a saxophone. The piano was in the centre and Shayna sat perched on the stool, her hands resting on the keys. Sammy looked for Moishe and found him on the bandstand talking to a heavyset man in a blue suit and a starched white shirt.

"Sammy, meet Izzy Thomasky, star of the Yiddish stage."

Sammy shook the man's outstretched hand. "Pleased to meet you."

"I hear you are a very talented young man," Mr. Thomasky said in a heavily accented voice. "So, you will sing with me tonight?"

"If you think I can," Sammy said. Suddenly his stomach felt like it was filled with butterflies.

"You can talk? Yes? So you can sing." Mr. Thomasky turned to the bandleader, who waved his baton in recognition.

People applauded. A few stomped their feet. Moishe stepped forward. "Ladies and gentlemen"—he turned to Mr. Thomasky—"you think we have any gentlemen here?"

Mr. Thomasky waved his hand. "Ladies maybe, but gentlemen?" Everyone laughed. He signaled the band and started singing.

The show was well underway. Sammy was on stage. Shayna played the piano and Adam and Joshua hid in the bushes at the side of the casino. Everything was in place. *The only thing we need is the horseman,* Sammy thought.

And then he heard it—hoof beats and a horse's whinny followed by the loud snap of a whip. The music stopped and people ran outside to see what was going on. Sammy jumped off the stage and joined them, followed by Shayna and Moishe. They stood on the lawn as a headless figure on a black horse with a white scar galloped towards the crowd.

Adam and Joshua ran out of their hiding spots and stood on either side of the incoming horse, banging on pots with metal spoons. Joshua blew high pitched blasts from a whistle clenched between his teeth. The panicked horse rose up on its hind legs, threw the rider to the ground, and galloped away into the woods.

"I know it's you, Nathan. Take off that ridiculous costume. I know you have a head, although I'm beginning to wonder if there is anything in it." Mrs. Liebman pulled off the rider's cape. Mr. Rothstein groaned and struggled to get up.

"Moishe! You set me up!" he yelled.

Everyone turned to look at Moishe. He raised his hands and shouted back, "No, no! I didn't have anything to do with it!"

As Mr. Liebman hauled Mr. Rothstein to his feet, Sherriff Miller made his way to Moishe. Sammy turned and ran.

"Sammy!" Shayna yelled. "Where are you going?"

Sammy didn't answer. He had seen Mr. Katzenblum sneaking away. He sprinted across the hotel grounds and caught up with him on the dock at the lake. He was untying the knot holding the rowboat to the piling.

Sammy spoke, "I know it's you. I know you're the mastermind behind the Headless Horseman."

Mr. Katzenblum turned and laughed. "I have no idea what you're talking about, young man."

"You want to buy the hotel." Sammy fished the envelope out of his pocket. "And I have proof."

Mr. Katzenblum looked shocked, recognizing the envelope. "Where did you get that? I demand that you return it this instant!"

"I'm going to have Sheriff Miller look at it first."

"So you think you've figured it all out? Such a smart boy." Mr. Katzenblum finished loosening the knot, dropped the rope, and stepped towards Sammy. "Too bad that letter won't do you any good if no one can read it."

He grabbed Sammy around the shoulders and shoved him off the dock.

CHAPTER THIRTY-TWO

SOLVING THE MYSTERY

Sammy gasped as he plunged into the water. It was cold. Everything was dark and only the dim light of the moon told him which way was up. He thrashed about, trying to get to the surface. His shoes were weighing him down, so he kicked them off. The water stung his eyes and he was sure he could feel fish nibbling on his toes.

Sammy closed his eyes and kicked as hard as he could. He broke the surface, quickly gulped in air, and, trying to recall everything Adam had taught him, swam towards the dock.

In the meantime, Mr. Katzenblum had climbed down the ladder and into the rowboat. Sammy reached the boat, grabbed onto the side, and tried to pull himself up. The boat tilted violently. Mr. Katzenblum swiped at Sammy with an oar but as he leaned over, he caused the boat to tip even further. He lost his balance and landed in the water, pushing Sammy under as he fell.

Sammy disentangled himself from the man's grasp. He swam to the ladder, climbed up, crawled onto the dock, and found himself looking up into the face of the Hermit.

The Hermit took Sammy's arm and helped him to his feet. "You okay, son?"

Sammy nodded, too winded to speak.

"And what have we here?" The Hermit turned and hauled Mr. Katzenblum, who was struggling to climb the ladder, onto the dock. "Well, well, well. Looks like I've caught me a big fish," the Hermit said, clutching Mr. Katzenblum's arm. "Let's all go to the hotel. There are a few people there who want to talk to both of you."

By the time they got to the casino, the crowd had thinned and Mrs. Liebman was guiding the last few stragglers off the porch.

"Sammy, what happened?" Mrs. Liebman looked at his shivering form.

"Mr. Katzenblum tried to escape in the rowboat and pushed me into the lake," he explained. "Where's Sheriff Miller?"

"He's got my dad, Moishe, and Mr. Rothstein in the casino. Are you okay?" asked Shayna.

"Is *he* okay? Look at *me!*" Mr. Katzenblum whined. He was drenched from head to toe. His white suit was dotted with bits of pond scum.

"Shayna, do you still have the real letter?" asked Sammy.

"Sure do," she said, pulling out a folded piece of paper from her skirt pocket.

"Why you…" Mr. Katzenblum lunged towards Shayna, but the Hermit held him back.

Sammy turned to Mrs. Liebman. "You're going to want to get Mr. Katzenblum in there too." He nodded at the casino door.

She nodded. "Okay, but first, let's get you a towel."

They never did finish the show. Before Mr. Thomasky left, he told Sammy that he was good performer and gave him a card, inviting him to come to the theatre on Second Avenue to see him perform when Sammy was back in the city. Maybe, he said, they could even do a number together. Now Sammy had two invitations, one from Mr. Thomasky for the Yiddish theatre and one from Eddie Cantor for his vaudeville show. But all that would have to wait until the fall. Now, they had to unravel the mystery of the Headless Horseman.

Everyone sat at a round table in a corner of the casino: The Liebmans, Moishe, Mr. Rothstein, the Hermit, The Ichabods and Sheriff Miller, who had handcuffed Mr. Katzenblum to a chair so he couldn't escape.

Aunt Pearl had wanted to stay, but Mr. Liebman had growled at her to "go away". Then she had pulled Joshua to his feet and ordered him back to his room, but Joshua had ignored her and plunked down in his chair. Aunt Pearl huffed out of the casino muttering that the sooner they left this place the better, and that she would start packing first thing the next morning.

Mr. Liebman opened the conversation.

"Will someone please tell me what is going on?"

"A joke." Moishe held out his hands. "A little joke to keep everyone amused."

"Yes, yes, a joke." Mr. Rothstein mopped his brow. "Some fun."

Mr. Liebman leaned across the table and glared at his brother-in-law. "You think that's funny? The truth! NOW!"

"You won't listen to reason," Mr. Rothstein spat out. "Things are changing. Katzenblum is an investor who will help us turn this place into a big hotel, but you and your wife are too stubborn to talk."

"So it was *you* who broke my dishes? *You* who ruined my strudel? *You* who put frogs in the pool? *You* who wanted to scare us out of here?" Mrs. Liebman shouted.

"No, that was all Moishe."

"Not the strudel! I don't mess with strudel." Moishe clarified.

She glared at Moishe before turning back to her brother. "You think, maybe, we are stupid? We will fall for your shenanigans? And you," she rounded on Mr. Katzenblum. "You are the big *macher*, the"—she spat out the word—"*businessman* who wants our hotel?"

"I am," Mr. Katzenblum said. "Why else would I spend the summer in this dump?" He sneered, waving his hand around the room. "But you see, *I* have imagination. *I* can visualize what it can become."

"Yes. Because someone from the Port Authority of New York and New Jersey tipped you off that they're building a tunnel under the river." Shayna shook the letter in her hand and passed it to Sherriff Miller. "You wanted to buy the land before its value went up."

Mr. Katzenblum immediately looked at Sammy.

"You're going to regret tricking me."

"You're in no position to be making threats," warned Sheriff Miller as he skimmed the letter. "Now, I suggest you cooperate."

"Mr. Rothstein, what gave you the idea to use the Headless Horseman?" Sammy asked.

Mr. Rothstein looked over at Mr. Katzenblum who rolled his eyes skyward.

"It was my idea," he said, adjusting his monocle. "The story is set in these mountains, and I believed bringing the ghost to life would be an effective way to accomplish my goals."

"But you wanted us to think it was Amos. That's why you used chalk to draw the same scar on your horse's shoulder that's on his horse."

"We knew people would eventually figure out the Headless Horseman wasn't actually a ghost. Amos already had a reputation for being a troublemaker. It wouldn't have been difficult for people to believe it was him."

"So you terrorized the Hermit so people would think it was Amos doing both?" Adam reproached him.

"It seemed like a good idea." Mr. Rothstein gave them a sheepish look.

Mrs. Liebman turned to the sheriff. "Sheriff Miller, you will maybe arrest these troublemakers?"

Mr. Rothstein held out his hands. "Rose, I'm your brother."

"With such a brother, I don't need enemies. So, Sheriff?"

"It's a good possibility," the sheriff drawled. "Anything you'd like to add, Moishe?"

Sammy watched as Moishe took a deep breath. Gone was his cocky self-assurance. He looked nervous and even a bit frightened. "Nathan was offered money for his farm, but only if he could get them," he pointed to the Liebmans, "to sell too. When they refused, we decided to try and scare them away."

Mr. Liebman patted his wife's hand. "See, Rose, I told you there was no ghost."

"Why were you terrorizing the Hermit?" Adam asked.

"We were against it, but Katzenblum refused to let him stay on that hill."

Mr. Katzenblum grimaced. "I was going to tear this dump down and build a grand masterpiece of a hotel. Do you honestly think my clientele would be comfortable with him next door?" He looked at the Hermit. "It's nothing personal. Just business."

The Hermit had remained silent up to this point. Now he stood up and glared at Mr. Katzenblum. "Ruining my garden, scaring my chickens, and dumpin' garbage in my well was just business?" he growled. His voice rose. "Setting my chicken coop on fire was just business?"

"Well, technically, Nathan handled that part."

Mr. Rothstein jumped in. "You wanted to set his *cabin* on fire! I had to convince you to set the coop on fire instead. Because I'm not a *lunatic*!"

"I had to do something. They do not understand the value of this property."

"Oh yes we do." Mrs. Liebman leaned over and wagged a finger in his face. "I understand that we have a place where people come to be happy. You want to build a palace for the rich. We want to keep the Pine Grove the way it is—for everyone who wants to enjoy the mountains and my good food! Humph! And you, Nathan," she turned to her brother. "For you to be involved with these crooks… our mother, may she rest in peace, would be turning in her grave."

Mr. Rothstein gave his sister a pleading look. "Tell me, Rose. Does this mean you don't want to sell?"

"Get out of here! As for you," she spun around to face Mr. Katzenblum. "Listen to me: *We are not selling our hotel to you or anyone else.*"

The sheriff spoke. "Mrs. Liebman, Zeke, do you want to press charges against these men? Destruction of property? Harassment? I have two empty cells in the jail."

Mrs. Liebman turned to her brother. "You are a disgrace to our family, Nathan, but I cannot send you to jail. What would Mama think of me? And you," she glared at Moishe. "You are no longer our tummler. Go play your tricks on someone else."

The Hermit looked from Mr. Rothstein to Moishe. "Y'all are just puppets in his big scheme. He's the real villain." He looked pointedly at Mr. Katzenblum.

Mrs. Liebman gestured at Mr. Katzenblum. "Him, I would like to look at through the bars of your cell."

"Mrs. Liebman," Sammy piped up. "You need new dishes. Pretty ones. And you can probably use new pots and pans. And the swimming pool could use a coat of paint." He turned to the Hermit. "And you want to see your daughter and your new grandson, right? Maybe build them a guesthouse for when they visit you?"

"So?" Mrs. Liebman raised an eyebrow.

Adam pitched in. "So let Mr. Katzenblum pay for all of it—the repairs and new equipment for the hotel, and the train tickets and new cabin for Zeke. Mr. Rothstein and Moishe can work for both of you until you think their sentence is done."

The sheriff looked impressed. "A fine solution, young men. What do you say, Mr. and Mrs. Liebman? Zeke?"

The Hermit chewed it over and then gave a firm nod. "It's going to be a very expensive cabin. And first-class tickets!"

Mr. Liebman stroked his chin. He looked at his wife. "I think it is a good plan. But it is up to you, Rose."

Mrs. Liebman was quiet for so long, Sammy worried she wouldn't agree. But then she smiled. "Yes. It is a good plan." She turned to the three men. "I want the best pots money can buy. And the meat dishes should have red roses on them. The milk dishes should have some kind of blue— maybe cornflowers. I think all the buildings and bungalows could use a new coat of paint and the front lawn needs to be weeded. As for the swimming pool…"

She was still talking as The Ichabods left the casino. Outside they paused and looked up as thunder rolled across the sky.

"Sounds like the Horseman is going home." Sammy laughed.

"This time, I hope he'll stay there. Come on." Shayna motioned for the others to follow her. "I know where Mama keeps the cookies. All this adventure has made me very hungry."

CHAPTER THIRTY-THREE

GOODBYE

"So, do you think that ended well?" Sammy asked when The Ichabods gathered near their rock after lunch the next day.

"I wish the Hermit had socked Mr. Katzenblum." Joshua punched the air with his fists.

They all laughed.

"I think it's time we forget all of this and start planning for Labour Day." Adam stood and walked over to the pool. "It's the day before everyone returns to the city and the Liebmans want to make it really special. Sammy, since Moishe isn't their tummler anymore, it's up to you to plan the program. Shayna and I will organize games for the children."

"What about me?" Joshua whined.

"You don't have to work because you're a guest," Sammy told him. "At least, that's what you've been telling us all summer."

"What if I don't want to be a guest?" Joshua pouted. "I want to stay with The Ichabods."

"That's okay with us. There's only one problem." Sammy tried to hide a smile.

"What's that?"

"Your mother."

"My mother!" Joshua wilted. "You can handle her for me, can't you, Sammy?"

"Uh uh." He looked Joshua in the eye. "You want to be an Ichabod, prove it. Go deal with the dragon lady."

For a moment, Joshua seemed to shrink to half his size. Then he straightened, and threw back his shoulders. "I will *tell* my mother that I am working this weekend."

"Good luck." Joshua left and Sammy turned to the others. "Dragons eat people, don't they?"

"Only if they taste good." Shayna giggled.

Adam grinned. "Then we don't have to worry about Joshua."

It was the first Monday in September—Labour Day.

Sammy's father and Tanta Martha had come up the day before to spend the holiday and then take him home. They brought good news. Malka had had her baby. It was a girl and Sammy could hardly wait to meet her.

When Sammy walked into the kitchen, Mrs. Liebman was taking fresh rolls out of the oven and Shayna was filling pitchers with sour cream.

"Everyone is up early." Sammy took the pitchers from Shayna and placed them on a cart. "I'll put these on the tables." He rolled the cart into the dining room where Adam was distributing dishes. "Good morning." He lifted a pitcher, wiped a drip off with a dishtowel, and placed it on a table. He paused and viewed the room. "I'm going to miss this place." He sighed. "I didn't want to come because I thought I'd be bored."

Adam laughed. "It certainly hasn't been boring." He leaned against a table and folded his arms. "I'd say this has been a pretty exciting summer. What will you do back in the city to top it?"

Sammy thought of the cards from Eddie Cantor and Mr. Thomasky that were tucked into his wallet. "I might go into show business."

"Save me a ticket when you're starring in the Ziegfeld

Follies. Now, Mr. Vaudeville, we'd better get these tables set before your Aunt Pearl and the other guests demand their breakfast."

The rest of the day went by as normal. After lunch, the guests and relatives gathered on the lawn for the afternoon's activities. Sammy's father and Tanta Martha came up to him. Papa regarded him with a frown.

"So, you have had an eventful summer. You are ready to come home?"

Sammy looked from him to Tanta Martha. Her face was partially hidden by a floppy brimmed hat and she was twisting a white lace handkerchief in her hands. When she looked at him, Sammy saw confusion in her eyes. *She's nervous about me coming home,* he realized. *We're both scared.*

"So?" Papa was waiting for an answer.

"Yes, Papa." Sammy took a step towards them. "I'm looking forward to getting to know you better, Tanta Martha." He smiled weakly.

"So am I, Sammy." She held out her hand. "We will be friends."

"Yes," he nodded and shook her hand.

Adam's voice interrupted them. "Okay, everyone," he

called through the megaphone. "Time for our sack race. The children crowded around him as he handed out burlap bags. Sammy helped them step into the bags and showed them how to hold the bags up with their hands. Adam counted, "one, two, three," and then blew a blast on his whistle. The children laughed and stumbled as they hopped across the grass to the lawn chairs marking the finish line.

Everyone clapped and cheered. A boy named Ze'ev, who had come up for the week with his parents, won. Sammy presented him with a blue ribbon, which he pinned to the boy's shirt.

Adam lifted the megaphone. "Now it's the adults' turn. Who wants to try? How about you?" He turned to Aunt Pearl.

"Me, jump around in that?" Aunt Pearl sniffed. As she retreated to the shade of the porch, Uncle Milton stepped forward.

"I'll play your game. Play, play, play." He accepted a sack from Adam and looked at the crowd. "Who will join, join, join me?"

"I will," Sammy said and took a sack.

"I will race too." Mr. Liebman joined them.

"And I."

Everyone gasped as the Hermit strode up to Adam. "Well, don't just stand there, give me one of those."

"Yes, sir." Adam handed him a sack. Three other men joined them.

"Ready? One, two, three…" Adam blew his whistle.

The race was on. Only this time, the men raced three laps, to and from the chairs. When the Hermit won, everyone applauded. He took the blue ribbon from Adam. "Thank you, folks," he grinned. He walked over to Sammy. "So, you're goin' back to the city tomorrow."

"Yes. I'm going to miss being here."

"What will you miss?"

"Everything." He looked into his eyes. "You."

"Me? Why me?"

"I like you."

The Hermit's face softened into a smile. "You're a good boy." He clapped a hand on Sammy's shoulder. "You've got a good heart. Them too," he said as the rest of The Ichabods joined them. "But you sure do cause a mess of trouble."

CHAPTER THIRTY-FOUR

GOING HOME

Adam and Sammy loaded Aunt Pearl's luggage into the wagon. "Hey, Joshua, don't just stand there. Help us," Adam said.

"I don't have to. I'm a guest."

Sammy rolled his eyes. "Some things never change."

"I was just kidding." Joshua picked up a valise and set it in the wagon.

Sammy looked at him, dumbfounded.

He returned the look. "Well, I *am* an Ichabod, aren't I?"

Adam shook his head. "Will wonders never cease." He gave Sammy a questioning look. "So, will you be back next summer?"

"If the Liebmans will have me."

"Of course we'll have you." Shayna came over and held

out a basket. "Mama baked these buns for your trip."

Sammy took the basket. "I'll visit you in the bakery in New York."

"That'll be nice."

"If you need help, I can work there sometime."

"What about your vaudeville career?" Adam teased.

"I'll do that too."

Aunt Pearl bustled up to them. "Vaudeville, *shmadeville*. Get in the wagon or we'll miss our train. Ruben, Martha, are you coming?"

Papa and Tanta Martha hurried up. "I was saying goodbye to Mrs. Liebman," Tanta Martha said. "I told her that I am a good baker, if she ever needs help."

"One of the best," his father added. Sammy looked at Papa. He was looking at Tanta Martha and his eyes were soft, like when he used to look at Mama. Sammy felt a tug at his heart. Papa was happy. That was the important thing to remember.

"Everyone take their seats." Aunt Pearl clapped.

"Yeah, get in," Joshua echoed.

"Yes, sir." Sammy saluted. He climbed up front beside Adam. Joshua sat beside him and their parents and Leah sat behind them. Adam flicked the reins. As the wagon lurched forward, Sammy took one last look at the Pine Grove. He thought of all the people he'd met that summer: the Liebmans, Moishe, the Hermit. He thought of how The Ichabods had worked together to accomplish something important. He was proud of what they'd done. He was going home stronger and feeling more grown up than when he'd left. He felt a tap on his shoulder. He turned his head and found Joshua staring at him.

"Hey, Greenie. When we get back to the city, remember, I'm still the boss."

"Sure, Joshua." Sammy pretended to ignore him. But Joshua poked him again.

"I mean it. I'm really the boss."

Here we go again, Sammy thought. *The Awful Joshua is still here.* And then he saw him grin and Sammy gave his shoulder a playful poke. *Well, maybe not* as *awful.* He leaned back in his seat and settled in for the ride home.

HURLEYVILLE
280 - 281

Dietary Laws Observed

City Phone

Tivoli 2 - 9697

Pine Grove Hotel

כשר בתכלית וכשרות

LOCH SHELDRAKE, N. Y.

P. O. Box 277

Dear Friend:

We are pleased to announce the Opening of THE PINE GROVE HOTEL under the personal management of the GOLDFARB BROS. FAMILY. This assures you the extra comforts and attention that make an enjoyable vacation.

You will like the PINE GROVE'S informal, friendly and immaculate atmosphere. We have on our premises for your enjoyment a private natural swimming pool of the most modern nature, the finest of cuisine, the most pleasurable of entertainment and all sports activities.

We extend a cordial invitation for you and your friends to come out and enjoy your vacation with us.

Sincerely,

Goldfarb Bros. Family.

P. S. THIS YEAR FOR YOUR GREATER COMFORT AND ADDED PLEASURE, WE HAVE NOW MADE MANY NEW IMPROVEMENTS.

Above: A brochure from the real Pine Grove Hotel

HISTORICAL NOTE

The earliest summers of my life were spent at my family's hotel, The Pine Grove, in the Catskill Mountains of New York. It was during World War II. My father was serving in the navy. My mother, along with her brothers and sisters, worked in the dining room while my cousins and I played together and enjoyed country life. The Pine Grove was much as I describe it. However, I've set the story twenty years earlier, at a time when the area was just being discovered by immigrant Jewish families as a haven where they could afford something they had never known, or even dreamed of, in Europe—a family vacation.

In the early 1900s, Jewish farmers who had settled in the region began renting rooms to people who wanted to get away from the city's summer heat. As more people flocked to the mountains, those boarding houses turned into hotels and bungalow colonies. By the 1950s, the area, which became known as the Borscht Belt (because the hotels served a beet soup called borscht) had become a flourishing tourist destination. There were hundreds of hotels, big and small, throughout the area. At resorts like Grossinger's, famous stars, a number of whom got their start there, entertained guests from all over the world. Although the golden era of the Catskills' has passed, the region's history and natural beauty continue to attract thousands of people every year.

Left: The author and her aunt on the pool deck at the Pine Grove Hotel.
Right: The author and her cousins on a swing in the yard of the hotel.

ACKNOWLEDGEMENTS

I want to thank the team at Fitzhenry & Whiteside for their faith in *Sammy and the Headless Horseman*. To Christie Harkin, my first editor, thank you for your patience and understanding when I had to stop working on the book for personal reasons. To Cheryl Chen, my editor who took over when I returned to the project, it was fun working with you. Your insights and suggestions were invaluable in helping me construct the puzzle that became the story of Sammy's ghostly summer at the Pine Grove Hotel.

Many writers have written about the Catskills. Washington Irving was an American writer who lived in the nineteenth century. His two most famous stories, "The Legend of Sleepy Hollow," and "Rip Van Winkle," are set in the Catskill Mountains and are so well known that they have become viewed as folklore. When I decided to make this book "spooky," I borrowed the idea of the Headless Horseman from "The Legend of Sleepy Hollow." So thank you, Mr. Irving.

Many of the details of life in the Borscht Belt came from the books *It Happened in the Catskills* by Myrna Katz Frommer and Harvey Frommer and *In the Catskills* by Phil Brown. That's where I learned about things like tummlers who entertained by jumping in the pool fully clothed and mountain men. And, of course, I grew up hearing the stories of my mother, aunts, and uncles and their time at the Pine Grove Hotel. While this story and all the characters are fiction, the memory of those days is real.

GLOSSARY

Boychick: an affectionate term for a young boy

Bubbie: grandmother

Gelt: money

Got in himmel: God in heaven!; said as an exclamation

Impresario: a person who organizes or manages public entertainments, especially operas, ballets, or concerts

Kiddush: a blessing made over wine

Macher: an ambitious person; a big shot

Mensch: a person of character; an individual of recognized worth because of noble values or actions

Meshegoss: inappropriate, crazy, or bizarre actions or beliefs

Meshugoyem: crazy people

Nudnik: a pest; a persistent and annoying person

Oy/Oy vey: "Oh, how terrible things are."

Pooh pooh pooh: a phrase said (in lieu of spitting three times) to ward off the "evil eye"

Schmaltz: fat

Shabbos: the Sabbath

Tanta: aunt

Tsoriss: suffering, woes

Tummler: an entertainer who goes from place to place